Jamie Rix

SCHOLASTIC

*For all my nephews
and nieces who
asked for more*

Scholastic Children's Books,
Commonwealth House, 1–19 New Oxford Street
London WC1A 1NU, UK
a division of Scholastic Ltd
London ~ New York ~ Toronto ~ Sydney ~ Auckland
Mexico City ~ New Delhi ~ Hong Kong

First published in the UK by Scholastic Ltd, 2001

Copyright © Jamie Rix, 2001

ISBN 0 439 99818 2

Typeset by M Rules
Printed by Cox and Wyman Ltd, Reading, Berks

10 9 8 7 6 5 4 3 2 1

Contents

Knock Down Ginger

It was a well-to-do private road in the town of Nimby. Barriers across either end restricted access to *Residents Only*. Mercedes, Jaguars and Jeeps lined the leafy drives while children played safely in the front gardens. This was millionaire's row, where money talked and where keeping up with the Fortescue-Smythes was what mattered, so that the oldest resident, poor old Mr Thrips, was despised for being different. His was the house with the boarded-up windows and peeling paint, the overgrown garden and cracked drains, the earth sculptures and beehives. His was the sore thumb, the carbuncle, the blot on the landscape. His was the house with the fat, flesh-eating flies in the dustbins; the house with the dung beetle's dung pile on the porch; the house with the wasps in the windows, the ants in the plants and the ticks in the bricks. His was the house they called Bug City Central.

Ginger Pie was a large, ungainly boy, with pale podgy cheeks and light red hair. He was so fair that at a glance you could be forgiven for thinking he was bald. He lived opposite Mr Thrips and just for the fun of it he and his best mate, Milo, a wild child with baggy trousers, devoted their spare time to wrecking the old man's life. It's what bullies do – persecute people who are different. They called him names. They yelled:

> "Bug Man! Bug Man!
> Squirt him with a spray can!"

while spraying his house with a particularly potent insect repellent called A Slow Lingering Death. They hung big notices on his front door that screamed *"Bug Off*!" They released his rare collection of dragonflies by smashing a window. They sprayed his flowers black to confuse the bees, and they filled an umbrella with snails, pushed it through his letterbox, shouted "snail mail!" and sprang the umbrella open so that the snails splattered in a slimy heap on his door mat.

"But why?" lisped Milo's little sister Elisa, who couldn't see what harm the old man was doing.

"Because," snorted Ginger, "he not only *does* weird things, but he *looks* weird too."

"Tho do you," said Elisa honestly. "You're tho pale, you look like Dracula jutht drank your blood."

"Shut up, Lizzie," barked Milo, "or I'll tell Ginger what your nickname is."

"No, don't!" she cried. Her tongue was too long for her mouth and flicked in and out of her lips. "You know I'm *not* a lizard! Oh bloomin' blatht, I've thaid it now! I'm *not* Lizzie the Lizard! I'm *not*!" And she started crying because she'd told Ginger what it was by mistake.

"He's a freak!" Ginger continued cruelly. "His back's all bent over like a beetle's, his eyes pop out like a fly's, and his head's all covered with thin bits of hair like a hornet's leg fur!" Then just to prove his detestation of Mr Thrips he ran across the road, scrambled up the rickety fence and shouted, "Insect maniac!" to the old boy's back while he was tending one of his soil sculptures.

"That's not nice," said Mr Thrips, without turning round. "Not nice at all, Ginger." The boy froze. How had he known it was him?

"He's probably got eyes in the back of his head," said Milo when Ginger told him.

"You know what that means!" Ginger gasped.

"Never thtick your tongue out when his back'th turned?" suggested Lizzie.

"He's not a man, he's an insect in disguise! Like a scorpion-fly or something!"

The children's mouths fell open. What a totally terrifying thought – living next door to a two-metre-tall scorpion fly!

4

"He has to go!" Ginger said coldly. "There's no room for human flies in Nimby!"

At that very moment, Ginger's mother, Mrs Amelia Pie, was reaching the same conclusion at a meeting of the Local Residents' Committee. She was Chairman.

"He has to go!" she shrieked from her position of power on the stage. "His house is a disgrace. It's filthy. He breeds insects in Tupperware bowls!"

Mrs Deacon raised her hand. "That reminds me," she said sweetly, "there's a Tupperware party round at my house next Tuesday evening. All welcome."

"Thank you, Kitty," said Mrs Pie, politely. "Much obliged."

Then in the blink of an eye she was spitting venom again. "I mean, his soil sculptures are a disgrace. They're five metres high, they hum like some gypsy's generator, they look like something unpleasant that a very large dog has left behind, and they block out my sun when I'm sunbathing!"

"If I might interrupt," interrupted Colonel Dithering. "Knowing a little of the Australian culture as I do, being a cricket and boxing-kangaroo enthusiast, I should point out that these structures are not, in fact, soil sculptures." (The meeting gasped. As Chairman of the Residents' Committee Mrs Pie was *never* wrong.) "They are termite mounds."

"Mounds of Termite?" she sneered, laughing at the absurdity of it. "I thought Termite came in jars."

"That's Marmite," coughed the colonel. "Termites are little white ants that eat houses."

Eat houses! Now here was an issue the committee could really get into a flap about.

"Prices crisis!" shrieked the Treasurer, causing an instant uproar.

"If the termites eat our houses who will buy them?" said one.

"Where will we park our cars?" said another.

"Who will come to our cocktail parties?" twittered a third.

"The solution is obvious," said Mrs Pie

decisively. "We must get rid of Mr Thrips and flatten his house to the ground."

"But where will we find someone to undertake such a disagreeable task?" fussed Mrs Deacon.

"I know just the person," smiled Mrs Pie.

"He'll have to be cruel, vicious and nasty!" said the colonel.

"Oh he's definitely that," smiled the Chairman. "He's a chip off the old block."

"Yes, but who is it?"

"My son," she said. "Ginger!"

All hysterical nonsense, of course. If anyone had bothered to ask, they'd have discovered that far from being a flea-ridden weirdo, Mr Thrips was a respected entomologist, who studied insects for a living. Nonetheless, Mrs Pie talked to Ginger, and Ginger talked to Milo and between them they came up with a devilish plan to run Mr Thrips and his termites out of town. They would play Knock Down Ginger.

For those of you unfamiliar with Knock Down Ginger, it is a puerile game played by puerile children with brains the size of tadpoles. That said, it *can* be quite fun, if your victim is the pits. But Mr Thrips was *not* the pits. He was the bee's knees and that makes all the difference. Basically, Knock Down Ginger involves ringing a doorbell and running away like a lily-livered coward before the door is answered.

The first time Ginger and Milo did it, it worked a treat. They crept up on the house, commando-style, and hid behind a bush while straws were drawn to decide whose finger should do the honours first. Ginger drew short. He took a deep breath, narrowed his piggy eyes, dashed up the drive, stabbed the bell and sprinted back to the bush as fast as he possibly could. He needn't have bothered. Mr Thrips was so old and infirm that it took him the best part of ten minutes to open the door. The boys marked his slow progress from the back of the house to the front by the sound of his tiny, frail voice.

"Coming," it whistled. "Don't go. I'm here. Coming!" When at last he opened the door his chest was wheezing. He was panting like a three-legged horse in the Derby. "Hello," his voice trembled weakly. "Is anybody there?" After taking a slow, painful look around he shut the door and went back inside.

Ginger and Milo sniggered like jackals. They gave him ten minutes to return to his armchair before Milo took his turn to ring the bell. Another ten minutes passed before a grey-faced Mr Thrips pulled open the door and slumped against the frame. "Hello!" He could barely speak, he was so out of breath. "I'm sorry it takes so long to open the door, but it's my aching bones. Hello! Oh, for a pair of wings!"

And with that he shut the door. And with *that* Ginger ran forward and rang the bell again, and so on and so on and so on all afternoon, until Mr Thrips was so exhausted that he could no longer walk. By the twelfth ring he was opening the door on his knees, by the thirty-third he was crawling and by the ninety-seventh he was dragging himself on his belly. "Yes," came the feeble cry. "Who keeps ringing my bell? What do you want?" But there was no reply, just the faraway sound of two poisonous toads croaking. Or was that giggling? Mr Thrips could not be sure.

"I've had an idea," said Ginger excitedly. "You keep doing the Knock Down Ginger bit at the front while I go round the back and knock down his termite mounds."

"OK," grinned Milo. "Why?"

"Because termites eat houses!" squealed Ginger, who thought his brain was bound to burst from having so many brilliant ideas. "And when they eat Thrips's house he'll have to move!"

He darted out from behind the bush, vaulted over the garden fence and landed right in the middle of the mounds. There were five, all dusty brown and grouped in a loose circle like Stonehenge. Ginger hadn't expected them to be quite so big. They were three times his height and towered over him like giant chocolate raisins. He put out his hand and touched the baked mud. It was vibrating. He pressed his ear against the dry crust. Deep down there was a faint humming noise, a stomping and crunching like distant soldiers marching, like an army of steel-booted ants on the move. A door latch clicked inside the house and Ginger spun round. Milo must have forgotten to ring the bell. Mr Thrips was in the kitchen. Now was *not* the time to termite!

With two giant steps, the fearless prankster was at the foot of the fence. One leap and he was over. A short run and he was back at the front door. A quick press and the doorbell was ringing for the umpteenth time. Only this time, Ginger did not run away. The old codger was in the kitchen at the other end of the house. He'd just seen him. He had at least ten minutes! Ginger put his ear to the door and gave Milo a cocky thumbs-up. But just as he did so, the door was ripped open and he was plucked off the step by a claw.

"Yes?" said Mr Thrips. They stood facing each other in the hall. Ginger was wondering how the old man had reached the front door so quickly. "What do you want?" Ginger was looking for the claw, but none was in evidence.

"I presume it's you who's been ringing my bell all afternoon."

The boy's mouth had seized up. He had just noticed that the walls, the floors and the ceilings were crawling with insects – crunchy ones, buzzy ones, stingy ones, leggy ones, diggy ones, snappy ones, sucky ones, nippy ones and pretty ones with wings.

"I said," repeated Mr Thrips with a steely glint in his eye, "what do you want?"

Ginger had a stag beetle on his shoulder and an earwig in his ear. "Erm. . ." He was finding it hard to concentrate.

"Then I'll tell you what *I* want," hissed the old man. "I want you to leave me alone, Ginger Pie. I want you *not* to ring my doorbell any more. I want you to buzz off and leave me in peace."

The insects buzzed loudly to reinforce what their master had said. The walls throbbed as they hovered on the wing and Ginger's top lip began to sweat. He thought he *would* go home after all. He didn't mind the crickets in his pockets or the ladybirds in his hair or even the woodlice in his nose, it was the cockroaches in his socks that he objected to.

But as he turned to go, he heard a faint humming noise coming from the other side of a closed door. It was the same noise he'd heard in the termite mound.

"Don't even think it," said Mr Thrips.

"Think what?" said a startled Ginger.

"There's nothing but danger there." Mr Thrips was spooking Ginger with his wide staring eyes and crooked neck.

"Where? What are you talking about?"

"Leave now, while you still can."

"What *is* behind that door?"

"I knew you wanted to know really," cackled the old man, stepping forward. "Oh all right, you've twisted my withered arm. I'll show you!"

"No," blurted Ginger. "I've changed my mind. I don't want to see it!" But Mr Thrips had already opened the door and was beckoning Ginger through with a lopsided smile as creepy as a crocodile's.

Standing in the centre of the empty room, surrounded by a misty halo of dust, was a white wooden chair. It was vibrating so fast that to the naked eye it didn't appear to be vibrating at all, rather like a dentist's drill.

"My termites are allowed out once a day for exercise," chuckled Mr Thrips, coughing on his own spit.

"Where are they?" asked the boy.

"Can't you hear them?"

"I can hear tiddly munching," Ginger said, "but I can't see a thing."

"You have to look with your imagination," Mr Thrips explained. "Allow your mind to wander *inside* that chair."

No! It couldn't be. It was incredible. "They can't be *inside* the chair?"

"Why ever not?"

"Because how did they get in?"

"From below," said Mr Thrips. "Didn't you know that termites eat from the inside out?"

Just then, a small piece of wood, no bigger than a coconut flake, was pushed out of one of the legs. The humming suddenly grew louder and a procession of white, bloodless ants poured through the hole like skydivers tumbling through the open door of a plane. The termites opened their translucent wings, streamed through the window and flew in single file back to their mounds in the garden.

"Is that it?" asked Ginger. "Have they eaten the chair?"

"Every last morsel," replied the entomologist.

"But how can they have done? It's still standing."

"Watch," said Mr Thrips, and he raised his right forefinger and brushed it lightly across the back of the chair. It instantly collapsed into a pile of sawdust. From the stunned look on Ginger's face, Mr Thrips could see that the boy was impressed. "They work from within," he explained, "and never touch the surface. They can eat an entire house and leave the outside looking completely untouched. So much so that nobody knows they've been there."

Ginger didn't believe him. "It must be a trick," he said.

"No trick," said the old man, as he showed the boy to the door. "Just the magical forces of nature. Now, do me a favour. No more Knock

Down Ginger, please, or I might have to play a few games of my own!"

Ginger found a nervous Milo sitting on the pavement with Lizzie.

"Thank heavens," he cried. "You've been gone hours. I thought you were dead."

"He was weird," trembled Ginger. "Those termites are his pets."

"Milo thaid that *I* could try Knock Down Ginger," lisped Lizzie excitedly. "He thaid it wath fun."

"No," said Ginger. "No more. It's not safe."

"Why?" Milo asked.

"Because they're not natural. They're like insects from another planet or something. They eat things inside out and they don't have blood."

Lizzie started to cry. "Can I change my mind?" she sobbed. "I don't want to be naughty any more!"

"Oh shut up!" barked Milo. "You're both a pair of scaredy cats."

Ginger flinched.

"Yeth I am!" bawled Lizzie. "And I don't care who knowth it!"

"I'm going back for another ring!" Milo said. Ginger was having a crisis. Milo was taking over and he didn't like it. The termites had been freaky, but Milo telling Ginger what to do felt wrong. Besides, what had seemed spooky in the old man's house now seemed rather silly in the cold light of day. How could Ginger Pie be scared of a few flying ants!

"Out of my way!" he snapped, pushing Milo and his sister to one side. "Let the Knock-Down-King through!" And with that he ran up to the house and rang the bell.

Only this time Mr Thrips did not come to the door. In the back garden, however, there was a frenzied buzz of activity, the ground trembled and the termite mounds thrummed.

Ginger waited for Mr Thrips for half an hour, ringing again and again and again, until eventually it wasn't much fun any more and he turned around and went home. He felt rather deflated. Knock Down Ginger was rubbish if the victim didn't come to the door. He put his hand in his pocket for his house keys, but he'd left them inside. He raised his finger and rang his own doorbell. Then he stood back and waited for his mother to open the door.

Ringing the doorbell was his first mistake. The sound waves filtered down through the ground and guided them in. Standing still was his second. It offered a target. It turned him from Standing Ginger into Sitting Duck.

Suddenly, the earth rumbled under Ginger's feet. It sounded like a distant underground train, or high-pressure water rushing through a pipe. It was racing across the road from Mr Thrips's house.

"From below." Two words. Those two terrifying words kept repeating themselves inside Ginger's head. They entered from below! He looked down at the path, but by then it was far too late. Now it was Mr Thrips's turn to play Knock Down Ginger!

It was quick and painless. The termites had had a lot of practice on chairs. Ginger felt an itching in his shoes, then a pricking in his heels and a strange thickening sensation that crept up his legs and spread through his body as if his blood had turned to sawdust. The termites left through his ears and made a beeline for the house.

Mrs Pie opened the door to find her son standing on the path like a statue, with a wide-eyed look of surprise on his face.

"Ginger. What are you staring at? Ginger!" She touched his cold cheek and he disintegrated in front of her into a pile of ginger dust. She screamed and ran back into the house, slamming the door behind her, shuddering the foundations and juddering the walls. By the time she'd reached the telephone her house had disintegrated too, and Mr Thrips's termites were folding their wings and settling down in their mounds to sleep off their unusually large supper.

The Upset Stomach

This is a terrible tale of neglect, which should serve as a warning to all of you children who want everything NOW! NOW! NOW! with no thought for the consequences.

Ethel was a greedy child. She was forever snacking. She never had one helping where two would do, and she was forever scheming to find new ways to eat more without being sick. Her parents, Mr and Mrs Turnip, had long since given up trying to curb their daughter's gluttony and nine times out of ten they gave in to her whims without so much as a whimper.

One winter, just before Christmas, Ethel read an article in the sports section of the newspaper about a company that was breeding stomachs for the annual Stomach Rolling Competition in Nether Wallop, Yorkshire. Sensing a glorious opportunity for double-gorging, she stood on the kitchen table and told her parents what she wanted for Christmas. "I want another stomach," she said. "I'll give it a name and carry it around with me wherever I go, so that I can eat twice as much food as I do now." Her parents looked faintly disgusted.

"But won't a stomach leave a mess around the house?" queried her mother. "With all those juices?"

"I'll keep it in a box," said Ethel, belching loudly as she finished her fourth rack of toast. "With airholes."

"And what does it eat?" asked her father.

"Everything!" scoffed Ethel. "It's a stomach, dumbo!"

"And does it need much looking after?"

"It needs walking every day so it doesn't get

fat. It needs food and water and it needs me!" she replied.

"So it's a bit like a pet dog," reasoned her father.

"No. It's a stomach," said Ethel. Her voice was tinged with disdain. "But if thinking of it as a dog will convince you to let me have one, I'll call it Rover."

Mr and Mrs Turnip had no answer.

"Good!" clapped their daughter. "Then that's settled. I'll phone up the farm and have one delivered." And that was that. That was all the thought that Ethel gave to buying a new "pet".

Two weeks later, the stomach was delivered.

"Whatever it is," sniffed the postman with the clothes-peg on his nose, "it don't half pong. And it hasn't stopped slurping and gurgling since it left the depot."

"It must be hungry," said Ethel.

"Is it a troll?" asked the postman.

"No," said the girl.

"Is it a jacuzzi?"

"No!"

"It's not a wee widdly pygmy treading grapes, is it?"

"Go away," said Ethel. "You are very stupid." And she took the sticky parcel from the postman and shut the door.

Mr and Mrs Turnip wanted to keep Ethel's present in its box until Christmas Day, but Ethel wouldn't hear of it. Without so much as a *Thank you* or *Do you mind if I do?*, she slid a paper knife under the lid and opened the box. The stomach was the size of a basketball. It looked like a grey jellyfish (without the tentacles, obviously) and made a constant sloshy sucky noise like two hippos kissing. Ethel lifted it out of its box and immediately dropped it on the floor when a tiny stream of liquid squirted out of a hole in the stomach's side and splashed the table.

"What was that?" she squealed, as the table cloth smoked and dissolved into a hole.

"Gastric juices," sighed her father, pointing to a warning on the box: **BEWARE! ACID! GASTRIC JUICES BURN!** From that moment on, Ethel liked her new stomach just a little bit less.

But come Christmas Day, the pet stomach performed to Ethel's satisfaction. When presented with food it did exactly what it had said on the box. The stomach and Ethel ate two platefuls of turkey, potatoes, sprouts, peas, bread sauce, stuffing, parsnips, sausages and gravy in ninety seconds. After scoffing all of the Christmas pudding – leaving nothing for her parents – two dozen mince pies, a tub of brandy butter, a box of chocolates and sixty-one dates, Ethel stretched out on the sofa and groaned. She was fit to burst. So was the stomach. It rolled away from the table gingerly, making tiny farty noises as it went and leaving a trail of gloopy goo on the floor. When it reached the sofa it looked up longingly at its new master, in a pathetically doggy sort of way, and bounced up on to Ethel's stomach, where it instantly collapsed into a full-bellied sleep. Ethel didn't have the strength to push it off, much as she would have liked to, and the two of them slept like logs through the Queen's Speech.

At five o'clock, however, the swollen stomach woke with a start and shoved itself into Ethel's face. The stench of decomposing food kick-started her brain. She shrieked and leapt off the sofa.

"I think it wants to go outside into the garden," said Mrs Turnip. The stomach jumped up and down as if to say yes. "Rather *urgently*!" she added.

"You take it," mumbled Ethel. "I'm too tired!" So her poor mother, who had done all the cooking and all the washing-up, had to carry Ethel's stomach into the garden, where it did what a stomach has to do behind the raspberries.

For the rest of Christmas Day and all of Boxing Day, the stomach was a perfect pet. It followed Ethel around the house, jumped up playfully when she stood still, and gurgled with pleasure whenever she deigned to look at it. But Ethel became irritated by its constant, doe-eyed attention. When she had asked for a stomach she hadn't realized quite how much tender loving care it would require.

"It's only trying to be friendly," said Mr Turnip.

"I think it's rather sweet," added her mother, who had a soft spot for poor defenceless creatures.

"Then it can sleep on *your* bed tonight!" moaned the girl. "I didn't get a wink of sleep last night with its rumblings and grumblings and little squeaky noises!"

"No thanks," said her parents, who had just invested twenty pounds in new sheets.

"And while we're on the subject," continued Ethel, "I'm not taking it for a walk again either. Passers-by sniggered at me! And when I hid it up my jumper three boys laughed till they split their trousers. They said I had the fattest stomach they'd ever seen. So I told them it wasn't mine and to prove it I pulled the stomach out from underneath my jumper. You should have heard the screams. They thought I'd disembowelled myself!"

"You should have thought of these things before you asked us to buy it," admonished her father.

"Well I'm thinking about it NOW!" sulked Ethel. "It's quite fun having two stomachs at mealtimes, but the rest of the time it's a complete load of poo!" The stomach could tell when it wasn't wanted. It slunk away into the corner and wept sad green tears of bile.

That night the unloved stomach slept in the garden in a makeshift kennel. Mr Turnip lined a cardboard box with clingfilm to stop its gastric juices leaking out and ruining his grass. But there was a heavy frost, and in the morning, when Mrs Turnip came out to feed it, the stomach was rock-hard and blue with cold.

"It needs warming up," she told Ethel. "Take it for a run."

"Do I have to?" whined the selfish girl. "Stomachs *can* run by themselves, you know!" But when her father threatened to stop cooking oven chips Ethel did as she was told.

*

The stomach looked like a hideously fat chihuahua and Ethel was filled with embarrassment and loathing as she dragged it round the park. Then all of a sudden she had a wicked idea. She placed the stomach behind a tree and told it to count up to one hundred while she went and hid. But this was no game of Hide and Seek. The moment she was out of sight Ethel sprinted home, abandoning the stomach to the foxes that lived in the wood. When she ran in through the kitchen door she made up a wild story about dogs attacking the stomach and eating it, and how extremely upset she was (which she wasn't really), and what a horrible colour last night's supper had been, and could she have another Christmas present? Suddenly the doorbell rang.

"Young lady left her Space Hopper in the park," said the smiling policeman, bouncing the stomach on the front step. Unfortunately, he bounced too hard, because the stomach guffed like a goat. "Phwoar!" he winced. "Think it might have a sprung a leak!" And with that he dropped the stomach and ran behind a tree to be sick.

Ethel was not happy to see her stomach again. She hated how feeble and helpless it was. She loathed the way it depended on her for everything. So early the next morning she packed the stomach into six plastic bags, caught a bus into the countryside and threw the stomach into a field of cows. It sank into the mud and gurgled plaintively, but Ethel felt no pity. She laughed cruelly and ran all the way home for food.

"Where's Rover?" asked Mrs Turnip later that night. "I've cooked its favourite meal."

"Dead," lied Ethel. "Don't talk to me about it. I'm grieving."

But the stomach was not dead. The stomach was hungry. Hungry for food and revenge. It tugged itself out of the mud and squirted a startled cow with its gastric juices. Then it ate her. *And* all her friends. *And* all the sheep in the next field. And by the time it had polished off the chicken farm and the dovecote on the other side of the road, the stomach was six metres tall and growing. It was a giant blob. It wobbled down the road like a huge jellied haggis, scaring cyclists into ditches and squirting acid at passing motorists. It rolled into the nearest village and terrorized the old folks, who thought it was the ghost of Winston Churchill. It squidged a vicar, picked clean the Pick Your Own Fruit Farm and drank all the beer in the pub. The giant stomach rumbled like an erupting volcano as it soaked the countryside with a shower of acid rain, laid waste to all that stood in its way and headed home to Ethel's.

It appeared on the six o'clock news.

"Killer Stomach on the loose!" sensationalized the reporter.

"Ugh!" shuddered an old lady in Lewes. "A loose stomach the size of St Paul's dome. What a smelly mess!"

"The stomach is angry!" the reporter went on. "It is what psychiatrists classically call an upset stomach."

"Well, I'm only glad it won't be me with a shovel in my hand!" muttered the old lady to her cat.

"The Prime Minister is taking no chances

and has sent in troops." But the stomach squirted acid at the tanks and their guns dropped off. In her heart of hearts, the PM doubted that the stomach could ever be stopped. It carved swathes of acid death through middle England and only came to a halt when it rumbled up to Ethel's front door.

"What do you want?" shouted Ethel. "Leave me alone!"

"I wouldn't speak to it like that if I was you," advised Mrs Turnip. "I think it's rather cross."

"I'm its master," the girl said. "It does what I say."

"Not any more," whispered her father, raising his eyes to the sky where the bloated stomach was blocking out the sun.

It rolled forward over the fence and spat at Ethel.

"I think it wants *you*!" trembled Mrs Turnip. "Oh whatever shall we do, dear? Why is it so upset?"

"I know," said Mr Turnip. "Maybe it's got wind." And he rushed inside to find his indigestion tablets in the hope that they might offer some relief. But by the time he came back out the problem was solved.

The stomach had eaten Ethel. It had sucked her up. It had got what it had come for and was now leaving town. But just as it reached the road there was a terrible gutsy rumble – a churning, bubbling, hot-spit growl that shook the earth to its core. Eating Ethel was the stomach's big mistake. The greedy girl was one mouthful too many. Like an exploding pig on a fairground stall, the stomach burst and covered the Turnips' house in fleshy shrapnel. Ethel had still not been digested and was expelled across the lawn. She shot through an open window and ended up on her own bed, dazed, bewildered and covered in bits of pink offal that smelled four times worse than a barrel of bad fish.

Ethel is no longer greedy. She hasn't got the stomach for food any more. You see, she still hasn't got that smell out of her nose, which means that *all* food tastes the same to her – offal!

Remember!
A stomach is for life, not just for Christmas.

The Gas Man Cometh

When telephones were first invented voices used to travel through underground wires that joined one phone to another. In those days, telephone lines were policed by moles, who had exceptionally good hearing on account of being blind. They would curl up next to the wires and listen to the talking voices. If they heard anything prank-like or sinister, all they had to do was catch themselves a shrew, pass on what they'd heard and send the shrew packing. The shrew in turn would tell a stoat, the stoat a fox, the fox a hound, the hound a horse, and the horse would hopefully have a friend who was a police horse and he could tell him. In this way a good number of criminal activities were nipped in the bud at the *"Slasher, I'm just telephoning to see if you're interested in doing a blag?"* stage.

But today it's far more complicated. As time moved on telephones became more sophisticated and moles were no longer any use. The police tried putting moles into orbit to eavesdrop on the sound waves bouncing off satellites, but moles can't breathe in space and all of them died. In fact the police got through several species of small, furry mammals before realizing that more sophisticated methods were required. Many now exist, including phone taps and bugs. Phone taps allow the police to listen in to villains singing in their baths, while bugs are highly trained talking insects that can crawl through telephone handsets, burrow into criminals' ears and report back on what they find in their brains.

And yet, for all this high-tech wizardry, the police still have no answer to the nuisance of telephone pranksters. Those faceless jokers – most of them boys – who think it's a wheeze to ridicule the old and infirm, to persecute those with unusual names, to shock and upset anyone who'll listen. And the reason the police have no answer to these telephone terrorists? They don't need one. Not with the Gas Man around.

A mobile phone was ringing when Mrs Krott gave birth to her only son, Stefan. It was the first noise he ever heard. The second was the midwife answering the call. Stefan could imitate twelve different telephone rings before he could talk. He could dial fourteen digits by the time he was eight months old and when he was one, his parents bought him his first telephone. It was bright red and yellow, made out of plastic and had an irritating Bugs Bunny voice that repeated "Thank you for calling me. Have a nice day!" every time Stefan replaced the receiver. He was quickly bored by it and turned his obsession to the real McCoy – the cordless telephone in the hall. Stefan would tuck it inside his nappy and take it out every few minutes to randomly poke the keypad. If the phone was ever answered he would stand stock-still and listen spellbound to the strange, high-pitched voice on the other end. "Hello!" it would screech. "Who's there? Hello! Who is this?" It made him laugh. But the more he laughed the angrier the voice became, and the angrier the voice became the more he laughed. Sometimes he was laughing for hours before his parents realized what he was doing and confiscated the phone.

But the more Stefan wound up strangers on the phone the more he found he liked it. By the time he was five he was making prank calls to the emergency services. He had the police out looking for a bugler. He had the RSPCA out hunting for a pelican crossing the road. He had an ambulance out searching for a man with a broken heart. And he had the fire brigade out to rescue a leaf from a tree.

"A leaf!" gasped the Fire Chief, standing at the bottom of the tree with two fire engines growling behind him. "But you said 'granny' on the phone. 'Help! There's a granny stuck up a tree.' Those were your exact words!"

"I meant leaf," giggled Stefan. "Sorry!" But the flashing lights looked brilliant!

When he was seven Stefan was such a nuisance that his parents locked every phone in the house and forbade him to use them. So he bought himself a mobile phone and used that instead. He phoned the grumpy school janitor and told him in a panicky voice that there was a horse in the gym!

"Quick!" he yelled. "Somebody might get killed! And bring a shovel. It's done a woopsie on the weightlifting mat!"

When he was eight, he phoned the headmistress and told her to prepare for a school inspection that very afternoon. She believed him as well, until he went too far and added, "By the way, give that nice Stefan Krott the rest of the week off. I went round to his house last night and inspected his schoolwork over dinner. He's very brainy and doesn't have to do sports if he doesn't want to!"

"Stefan," she replied. "Come and see me in my office now."

When he was nine he phoned the dinner ladies and pretended he was Michael Caine.

"My name is Michael Caine and I am in the

area, ladies, and when I say I fancy a spot of lunch, I mean it. Can you oblige? Oh yeah. Steak will do lovely. With chips. And a nice bottle of Beaujolais." And when Michael didn't turn up, much to the dinner ladies' disappointment, Stefan did them a huge favour and ate Michael's steak for him.

It was about this time that Stefan received *his* first phone call. I say call, it was more of a sinister silence, actually. He was at home, not doing any homework and spending his free time annoying perfectly nice people with unfortunate names, when a clicking on the line interrupted his prank call to Mr Stinky.

"Hello?" said Stefan as the ringing tone cut off. "Is anybody there?" He heard breathing at the other end. A finger scraped across the mouthpiece. A sticky throat swallowed. "Hello. What do you want?" Then suddenly the dial tone resumed and the phone was answered by an elderly man.

"Good evening," Stefan said. "Are you stinky?"

"Yes," came the frail reply, because the old man *was* Stinky. That was his name.

"Who is it?" asked his ninety-year-old wife from her armchair.

"It's a chap wants to know if I'm Stinky, dear."

"Well tell him you are," she shouted. "Don't keep him hanging on, wasting his time. Young man like that, he's probably important and busy."

"I am Stinky," said the old man.

"And is your wife stinky too?" continued Stefan.

"She is," he replied. "We're both Stinky."

"You should take a bath then!" At which point Stefan split his sides while Mr Stinky completely missed the joke.

As to his own phone call, Stefan thought that had been a joke too. Either that or a wrong number, and even if it *was* something more sinister, he was having far too much fun to stop now!

"Hello!" he said in his best Liverpudlian. "I'm from the Electric Company, like. Just checking everything's all right."

"Yes, thank you," said the unsuspecting voice at the other end.

"So the electricity's getting through then?"

"I think so."

"Telly working?"

"Yes."

"Telephone OK?"

"Seems to be."

"Is your fridge running?"

"Oh yes."

"Well what are you doing on the phone then? Run after it. Catch it before it escapes!"

Stefan was a master of deceit. He could lure a victim on to his hook without the victim ever knowing it had happened.

"Hello. Can I speak to Sarah Walls please?"

"No," came the hesitant reply. "There's no Sarah Walls living here."

"No Sarah Walls," Stefan muttered. "Tim Walls then. Is Tim Walls there?"

"I'm afraid he's not, no. I live here."

"I get it. With Imogen. Can I speak to Imogen Walls please?" The man at the other end of the line laughed.

"No. There's just me. There's no Imogen."

"Can you tell me when she'll be back then?"

"Never. She doesn't live here."

"What about Oscar Walls?"

"I think you've got the wrong number. There's nobody here but me."

"So you've got no Walls in that house at all?"

"That's right. That's what I've been telling you."

"So how does the roof stay up then?"

Stefan was the best! Or the worst, depending on which end of the telephone line you were standing.

He received his second call while his parents were out of the house. He was dialling a vegetarian when the tone cut dead as before, only this time the silence was broken by a whispering voice on the other end. It was so soft that Stefan had to strain to hear it.

"Stefan," it hissed. "We've got your number." Then there was a pause, just long enough to send a shiver up Stefan's spine, and he was reconnected to his vegetarian.

"Hi. Can you hear me when you're on the loo?"

"No," she said.

"Really? Because I can hear *you*."

Anyone else would have thought it strange that the whispering voice on the other end of the line had known Stefan's name, but not Stefan. He had ceased to think. He had become a crank call junkie. He *had* to have his daily fix of mischief. He *had* to hoax. He *had* to play his childish joke on the newly married couple.

"This is the police here."

"Oh dear," they trembled nervously. "What is it?"

"Just phoning to see if you've been burgled recently?"

"No. No we haven't."

"Oh. Would you like to be?"

"I beg your pardon?"

"It's just that we've got a couple of officers in your area tomorrow. They could pop in while you're at work, turn the place over, leave it in a right old mess. You won't even know they've been there. Interested?"

"Of course not!"

"It's all the rage. It'll give you something to talk about at parties."

"Look, who is this?"

"It's the police. We've been told to increase the number of crimes we solve. If we could actually know who did it *before* it's done, there's a fairly good chance we might actually catch the culprits."

"Are you really a policeman?" they asked.

"Are you really a thicko?" he replied, mocking them with hoots of scornful laughter and slamming the receiver down.

The phone rang instantly. There was no pause. It was as if the person ringing knew exactly when Stefan had finished his last call.

"Yes," said the boy, as he gingerly placed the receiver against his ear.

"Is that you?" hissed the same whispering voice at the other end of the line.

"You'll have to speak up. I can't hear you properly."

"Good. I don't want you to know who I am."

The hairs on the back of Stefan's neck stood up.

"Why not?" he asked cautiously, but his question was ignored.

"This is business," came the ice-cold reply. "Do you want to buy some helium?" There was a pause.

"Is that Mr Stinky?"

"No, Stefan, this is not Mr Stinky. I'm dealing with business. I am the Gas Man!"

"Who?"

"Are you deaf?" barked the voice suddenly. The boy was confused.

"No," he said, hesitantly. "What's helium?"

"A gas, Stefan. A hoot too! It's lighter than air, that's what it is. Fill a balloon with helium, it floats! Are you a balloon, Stefan?"

"What?" said the boy.

"Ha-ha," droned the Gas Man, flatly. "That was a good joke. I thought you liked a good joke, Stefan."

"I do," the boy said, "but why would I want to float? I want to make prank phone calls, that's all."

"Really?" chuckled the Gas Man. "Did I forget to mention that helium also changes the pitch of your voice and makes it squeak?" Stefan pricked up his ears. "Think of the potential. With a squeaky voice you could be Mickey Mouse, an alien from outer space, a jockey. . ."

". . .or the Queen!" Stefan cried with excitement. He had always wanted to impersonate the Queen on the phone, but he couldn't get the whine. Now he could. "I'll take it," he yelped.

"Yes," said the Gas Man, "I thought you would." Then, in a brooding voice that cut through the silence like razor-wire, he whispered, "You never had a choice."

The next day Stefan bunked off school. He doubled back from the bus stop and hid outside his house until his parents had gone to work. Then, he slipped inside and waited by the front door for his helium to arrive. At ten past twelve he heard footsteps on the path. The doorbell rang. Through the frosted glass Stefan could see huge shadows looming. He opened the door to three men in dark glasses. One was wearing a black suit, one was wearing a blue suit and the third was wearing a pair of yellow overalls. He was standing between the other two, who were so tough and grizzled that they could only be his bodyguards. In his hands he held a cylinder of gas.

"I am the Gas Man," he said, smiling creepily. "This is Mr Black and Mr Blue. Please do not excite them. Their names have been carefully chosen." Stefan tried to peer at the Gas Man's face, but the stranger pulled the peak of his baseball cap down over his white, hairless chin. "I have brought your helium."

"How much is it?" enquired Stefan as he grabbed the cylinder.

"It's free," said the Gas Man, which made Stefan rather suspicious.

"Why?"

"Why not? I like a joke as much as the next man." And with that the Gas Man clicked his fingers, the bodyguards turned on their heels, and the three gangsters swaggered down the path with their rear ends waddling like a family of ducks.

Stefan could not wait to get started. Instructions on the side of the cylinder told him to breathe in several mouthfuls of helium and wait for the squeakiness to begin. It worked a treat and a couple of minutes later Stefan was on the phone making a right royal nuisance of himself.

"Queen here!" he squeaked. There was a silence on the line.

"I beg your pardon?" said a shocked female voice. "Did you say Queen?"

"We did. Who's that?"

"Millie, ma'am." The helium voice was a perfect match to Her Majesty's.

"I want to have tea with a commoner, Millie. Are you common?"

"Not really, no."

"But will you be common round the teapot when we come?"

"If you'd like me to, Your Majesty."

"Call me Auntie Liz," said Stefan, trying desperately not to laugh. "Have you got cats? Because we *will* be bringing the corgis too. *And* one's husband. But don't worry, they're all house-trained. If one's husband makes a fool of himself on the sofa you can put him in the garden. Ooh, that reminds me."

"Yes, Auntie Liz?" said Millie.

"We could come at any time, so start cleaning right away. Dust the house from top to bottom."

"Certainly, Auntie Liz. Anything else?"

"Uncork the sherry and clear out the garage so we've got somewhere to park one's horses." At this point Stefan's belly hurt so much from suppressed giggling that he had to hang up. Helium really was a gas! He took another huge blast, picked up his mobile phone and dialled a new number.

"Hellair! Queen here! Would you like to buy Australia?"

And so it went on, all afternoon. Every five minutes another shot of gas, every five minutes another clueless victim falling for his royal ruse. What Stefan didn't notice however, was that with every mouthful of helium his feet rose further and further off the floor. The gas was making his body lighter than air. So much so, that three hours later, when he was in the middle of his fifty-sixth call, he took off, flew through the window and floated up into the sky.

"That's right," he squeaked, not noticing that he was passing through a cloud, "we're Her Royal Majesty the Queen! And we've had a portrait of oneself stolen from Buckingham Palace. Little one. Perforated edges. Drawn on sticky paper. Have you seen it?" High-rising Stefan clipped an aeroplane's wings as he chortled up his sleeve.

"This portrait," said the gullible person on the other end of the phone, "does it look like a stamp?"

"It does!" trilled Stefan's Queen.

"Then I have it!" cheered the victim.

"In that case, don't move," yelled Stefan as he floated past the stars. "I shall send the horse and cart right away!"

"Horse and cart?"

"To take you to the Bloody Tower, you nasty, bloody thief! To chop your stupid little head off!" Stefan hung up and mopped the tears of laughter from his eyes.

When he looked up, it came as something of a surprise to find himself floating in outer space. It wiped the smile clean off his face. Just then, an orbiting mobile phone satellite bumped into his back. Stefan grabbed hold of one of its aerials and clung on for dear life.

"Help!" he screamed. "Help!"

But there was nobody around for millions of kilometres. Not a single *human* ear could hear him.

His mobile phone rang.

"Yes," he trembled.

"Game over!" squeaked the helium-filled voice on the end of the phone. "You lose!" And then the phone went dead, which meant that Stefan could never make another phone call in his life.

He's still up there, still orbiting the earth, still clinging on to that mobile phone satellite. So now you know. When a teeny tiny voice interrupts your telephone conversation, it's Stefan. But whatever you do, don't believe a word he says.

The Urban Fox

Once upon a time, in a busy inner city not a million miles away from where you are sitting now, there lived a fox. His name was Elvis. Elvis had been born and bred in the city. He had never ever seen the countryside and had never killed a lamb or eaten a fresh chicken in his life. He lived quite comfortably in a semi-detached den that he'd dug underneath a garden shed. The shed belonged to Mr and Mrs Smith, an elderly couple with a small, snuffly daughter called Parker. Parker and Elvis were firm friends and liked nothing more of an evening than to sit on the pavement in the rush hour and watch the sun go down through the purple haze of exhaust fumes. Elvis loved the city. He was thrilled by the noise and excitement and eating his food out of a cardboard box. He was a fast-food junkie and would spend his nights hunting for take-aways in local dustbins. He was a thoroughly urban fox, who never once pined for the fresh air and open fields that lay beyond the gasworks.

One day a new couple moved into the street. They were obviously rich, because five removal lorries blocked the street while their furniture was unpacked. They drove a huge black Jeep with a sticker in the window that said *"Hunters Do It On Horseback!"* and they went by the names of Lord Percy Blunderbuss and Lady Davinia. He had a face like a tomato – all round and red with a green hat on top that looked like a stalk. She had wild, wispy hair that sat on her head like a large twist of blue candyfloss and a loud, piercing voice like a foghorn.

Elvis and Parker watched the unpacking of the lorries from the safety of the front porch. They had never seen so much furniture in their lives. Apart from the usual wardrobes, chests of drawers and Van Goghs, there were five gun racks, several tack boxes and a large metal case marked DEATH TRAPS – OPEN WITH EXTREME CARE.

"What do you think they want those for?" asked Parker.

"Don't ask," gulped Elvis, catching his breath suddenly. "Look over there!" He pointed to the last lorry, which had just rolled up its rear shutter to reveal six shiny horses and a pack of beagles. "What do they want *those* for?" he cried. The two friends could only wonder.

All was revealed at breakfast the following morning, when Mr and Mrs Smith received a visit from Lord and Lady Blunderbuss.

"Hellair," boomed the lord on the doorstep. "Pleased to make your acquaintance and all that, what! New in the area. Just getting to know the natives. Check out the lie of the land. This is the little wife, by the way."

"Hellair," screeched Lady Davinia. "Charmed, I'm sure."

"Thing is," continued Lord Percy, screwing a

monocle into his eye, "got to sort out the old sporting business now, what! Wondered if you could assist."

"We're not really sporty people," said Mr Smith.

"Unless you count Bingo," added Mrs Smith meekly.

"Bingo!" shrieked Lady Davinia. "Oh, how common. Not our sort of thing at all. Is there a stag hunting club round here?" The Smiths shook their heads. "Or pheasant shooting?" They shook them again. "Or bear baiting?" At the third shake, Lord Percy looked rather disappointed.

"You silly old trout!" he snapped at his wife. "I told you we should never have moved to the city. They don't understand that for a sport to be a real sport there's got to be killing. Still, no point in crying over non-spilled blood, what! Make the best of a bad job, and all that! Socks up!"

"Have you got servants?" Lady Davinia asked suddenly.

"Er . . . no," said Mrs Smith.

"Thought not. This house is filthy. Smells worse than a horse's stable."

"Still, can't be helped," added Lord Percy. "You're probably rather poor, aren't you? Mind if we take a look around?" He didn't wait for an answer. The pot-bellied lord and his horse-faced wife simply pushed their way through the hall and disappeared into the kitchen.

Now, it was not unusual for Elvis to join the Smiths for breakfast. Mr Smith couldn't eat crusts on account of him having no teeth and Elvis loved crusts, especially if Mrs Smith dabbed them first with fish paste. So imagine the surprise on the new neighbours' faces when they barged into the kitchen and saw a small girl and a red animal sitting at table with stripy napkins tied around their necks.

"Gadzooks!" shouted the lord. "It's a fox!"

"Vermin!" shrieked the lady. "Lock up your slaughters, I mean daughters, I mean sheep!" Lord Percy grabbed Mr Smith by the arm and pulled him into a corner. "I say sir," he whispered gruffly. "Dashed rum do here, what!

Did you know you've got a wild, scavenging fox scoffing your marmalade?"

"That's Elvis," said Mr Smith.

"I don't care if it's the Big Bopper and the Bluenotes, it's got to go! No place for foxes in a civilized society. Not clean, you see."

"What do you mean, got to go?" said Parker. "He's my pet."

"Was," interrupted Lord Percy, "*was* your pet, princess. Leave it to the lady wife and I. We know what to do." He tapped the side of his nose like a spy giving a secret signal.

"What are you going to do?" shouted Mrs Smith as the Blunderbusses shot out into the street.

"Tally-ho!" came the distant cry from the pavement. "Frock up!"

It was half an hour later when the bugle sounded. The Smiths went to the kitchen window and looked out across the small city gardens. Mrs Smith gasped at what she saw. Lord and Lady Blunderbuss had saddled up two horses. They were sitting astride them wearing bright red coats and long black boots. Lord Percy was drinking brandy from a hip flask and slapping his thigh with a whip. Now, bear in mind that this would have been a normal sight in the country, but in the city, in a twelve-metre garden surrounded by a brick wall, it was an extraordinary sight. It was made all the more bizarre by the pack of hounds that was milling around the horses' hooves, yowling and yapping in anticipation of a feeding frenzy.

"They're going fox-hunting!" exclaimed Mr Smith. "I don't believe it."

Mrs Smith shook her head and tutted her disapproval. "These country folk," she said, sadly. "They've got no idea. There's not enough space for horses and hounds in our little back gardens."

"I expect they'll jump over the fences," said Mr Smith.

"There'll be trouble if they trample my begonias," warned Mrs Smith. "I shan't stand for it." Just then Elvis padded over and joined them at the window. "Oh, listen to me," she apologized. "Here's me going on about my flowers and it's you they're hunting to death!" She rubbed the fox's ears. "What are we going to do to save you?"

"Don't worry about Elvis," said Parker, hugging her best friend's neck. "Those are country hounds and this is a city fox. They'll never catch him. He's far too street-wise." Parker winked at Elvis and Elvis winked back. Then the urban fox flicked his bushy red tail and shot out through the cat flap to meet the hounds head on.

Four gardens down the bugle sounded for a second time. The hounds howled like the devil was in them, the horses whinnied and reared up on their back legs, Lady Davinia shouted "Whoa!" and Lord Percy cried "Tally ho!" The ground shook as the hunt moved off. The beagles poured over the first garden fence like a spotted brown waterfall, followed by the large horses whose heavy hooves skidded across the neatly-trimmed lawn and tore up the grass.

Foxes are the most cunning creatures on earth and Elvis was no exception. The gardens were too small for him to run away and hide, so his plan was to make himself invisible by blending in with city life, in the hope that the hounds would run straight past him.

In the first garden, he found a piece of old string which he tied on to a stick. Then he stood like a statue next to a family of gnomes who were fishing in the goldfish pond. The hunt streamed by without so much as a second glance.

"They've got the fox's scent!" bellowed Lord Percy, foaming slightly at the mouth.

In the second garden, Elvis slipped on a bikini, a pair of dark glasses and a sun hat, and lay on a lounger by the swimming pool with a good book and a fruit cocktail.

"Hellair!" waved Lady Davinia as she galloped past. "Lovely day for it!"

In the third garden, Elvis outshone himself. He curled himself into a circle by clutching his tail between his teeth, hung on to a brick wall and pretended to be a satellite dish. The dogs stopped and sniffed and whined and barked, but they couldn't see him.

"Onward!" bellowed Lord Percy.

By now the hunt had left a trail of destruction behind it that stretched as far as the eye could see. Fences were knocked down, flowerbeds were flattened, children's climbing frames were twisted out of all recognition. There was a punctured paddling pool, a cracked patio, a bent barbecue and one unlucky potting shed that had collapsed under the weight of Lady Blunderbuss and her leaping horse.

The fourth garden belonged to a family with children. It was full of games – table tennis, croquet, miniature golf and a half-size football goal. Elvis thought about disguising himself as a tennis ball, but decided he was too big. He thought about disguising himself as a golf club, but couldn't work out where to hide his tail. He even thought about disguising himself as a penalty spot, but he couldn't make himself flat enough. In the end he disguised himself as a croquet hoop, and did such a good job that the dogs ran right underneath him.

"Blast that fox! Where is he?" thundered Lord Percy in his fury.

In the fifth garden, the cunning urban fox pretended to be a burglar and the hunt sailed by as if a burglar was the most normal sight in the world.

"I'm getting rather tired," complained Lady Davinia.

In the sixth garden, Elvis disguised himself as a birdbath. In the seventh, as a crunchy-munchy machine for chewing up weeds and leaves. In the eighth, as a shopping trolley. In the ninth, as a wheelbarrow, and in the tenth and final garden, as a rotating washing line, which fooled the hunt completely.

By now Lady Davinia was too exhausted to carry on, and her husband was panting like a hot dog on a summer's day. The hounds had collapsed inside a greenhouse, their pink tongues drooling over the tomato plants, and the horses had sat down and were refusing to jump any more fences. Elvis had beaten the hunt and Lord and Lady Blunderbuss were furious.

"Dashed city gardens!" blasted the lord. "We'd have caught that scoundrel in the country!"

"Hear hear!" agreed his lady wife. "I don't like the city at all. Too small. Too many places for foxy to hide. I want to go home, Percy."

"Me too, old girl. Back to the country, where there's space to kill whatever we please." And with that the snotty new neighbours trotted back to their house, packed up their belongings and drove away.

Elvis was a hero. Mr and Mrs Smith threw a huge street party to celebrate the lord and lady's departure, and all the neighbours were invited. They raised their glasses to the cunning urban fox and congratulated him for ridding the street of country vermin. "They deserved to be run out of town," said Parker. "You taught them a lesson, Elvis. Nobody can come into our little city and destroy our gardens!" And while everybody cheered Elvis blushed redder than his bushy tail.

A few weeks later, Lord and Lady Blunderbuss received a letter from the police. It informed them that they were wanted in connection with a large number of unpaid bills for damage caused by their reckless city fox-hunt. They fled to Scotland, where they're still being hunted now.

Spoilsport

It stood out like a sore thumb. It was a grubby little house on a pretty little street, and was lived in by the meanest family in Britain. They were called the Pinchguts. Ma and Pa were even too mean to give their children names, so they called them Girl and Baby. Baby was only six and still had a lot to learn about being mean, but Girl was ten and was already as mean as her parents.

Their house was a disgrace. Ma and Pa had not spent a penny on it since they moved in. That was twenty years ago. The roof leaked, the cellar flooded, the windows were so black with dirt that curtains were not required. When their landlord told them to decorate the house or get out, they used custard to save on paint and the tail end of a squirrel to save on a paintbrush. When they needed running water, they stuck a hose-pipe up their neighbour's plug-hole and stole his bath water. They burnt the furniture for firewood, stripped the wallpaper for loo paper, and used Nan's false teeth as rat traps! As for food, the Pinchguts did not believe in buying food when they could eat like kings from their own garden. Snail stew was a favourite, as were grass pizza, fox chops, worm bolognese, nettle meringue pie, toad in the hole (because a hole costs nothing), and the family favourite, magpie mousse. Pa Pinchgut had made a trap for catching birds. He smeared superglue on top of the nut dispenser. Now, just how mean is that?

If Pa Pinchgut wanted the lawn cut, he went up to the farmer's field at midnight and stole six sheep. He chased them down the road by terrifying them with pictures of lamb chops. Then, he locked them into his back garden and when they'd eaten all his grass, he phoned up the farmer in a furious funk and demanded compensation for the damage the sheep had done to his cherished lawn! They also saved money on shoe leather by making their children hop, skip and jump to school, which meant fewer contacts with the pavement, thereby reducing wear and tear on the soles. In wet weather they fixed water-skis under Girl and Baby's shoes, and pushed them out into the road to steal a tow off a passing truck.

Growing up surrounded by such meanness it was little wonder that Girl was such a mean-spirited spoilsport. She couldn't bear it if people were enjoying themselves. She had to wreck the fun. At parties she would shout at the magician, "I saw you put that card up your sleeve!" Or if there was a ventriloquist, she'd jump up and stick a bulldog clip on his lips. "OK, Mr Clip-Lips, *now* let's see your dummy talk!"

At birthdays she adored telling Baby what his present was before he'd opened it.

"It's a bald tyre for a 1975 Ford Cortina."

Baby stopped tearing the wrapping paper and started to cry. "Boo hoo!" he whined.

"That's a horrible present. I don't want a tyre."

"No, but I do," said Pa. "That's why I bought it. Give it here."

"Why do you want a tyre if we don't have a car?" sulked Baby.

"I'm saving for one, ain't I?" grinned Pa. "At the moment I've only got one bald tyre, but when I get the rest of the parts I can build me own."

At Christmas, Girl loved ruining the magic. Before she took Baby to see Father Christmas in his grotto, she wound him up for hours, saying things like, "Which lucky boy's going to meet Father Christmas and get loads and loads of presents then?" But when they were in the queue and Baby was next up on the knee, and was so excited he was nearly wetting himself, she casually said, "Course that's not Father Christmas, you know. That's Mr Collywobble from the ironmongers." And then when Baby's bottom lip started to quiver, she added. "If you don't believe me, tread on his toe. He dropped a hammer on it last week." So Baby trod on Father Christmas's toe and Father Christmas yelled, "Yow!" from where the hammer had bruised him. And because it was so funny seeing Father Christmas swearing and all the little children crying, Girl carried on.

"Go on. Tug his beard. It's false."

"Yow!" howled Father Christmas as the elastic snapped into his chin and Girl went for broke.

"And punch the elf. It's not real!" But the elf *was* real and punched Baby back, which meant that Baby cried all through Christmas. But the meanest thing that Girl ever did was to tell her Nan that she had a surprise party the following week to celebrate her ninety-eighth birthday.

"But it's not a surprise any more," groaned her disappointed grandmother.

"Whoops," Girl smirked. "Sorry. I thought you should know who's coming."

"Why?" asked Nan.

"Because nobody is! We invited a hundred people, but they all said 'No'. None of them can stand you."

"Oh stop!" gasped the frail old lady, "or you'll break my heart!"

"About time," said Girl. "We were rather hoping that might happen soon. You have made out your will, haven't you?"

Would it surprise you to know that Girl Pinchgut had no friends?

Then one night, Baby lost a tooth. He was eating supper – newt nuggets and mashed marigolds – when his tooth fell out on the table.

"Oh ssssuper!" he whistled, as his tongue poked through the hole. "That means I'll get money from the tooth fairy!"

"Ha!" snorted Girl. "What planet were you born on, Mr Gullible? Fairies don't exist!"

"They do. How could wishes come true if they didn't?"

"It's all done with mirrors!" she said snottily.

"The tooth fairy can't leave money under my pillow with mirrors," riposted Baby.

"No," sniggered Girl, "because the tooth fairy doesn't leave it at all!" But Baby refused to believe her, and when he came downstairs the following morning with a fifty-pence piece in his hand, Girl was taken aback.

"See," said Baby. "The tooth fairy did come. She left me fifty pence!"

"Grow up," snarled Girl. "She doesn't exist. That's Ma and Pa that is. They put that money under your pillow."

Ma and Pa looked surprised.

"No we didn't," Ma said. "Pa and I never give you money. It's ours! Why would we give it to you when we could spend it on ourselves first?"

"They're just saying that to stop you from crying," said Girl nastily. "Don't listen to anything they say, Baby. Your childhood stops here. The tooth fairy's dead!"

At that precise moment, in an insubstantial reality beyond the bounds of Reason, the tooth fairy was pouring cauldrons of boiling fluoride toothpaste over the battlements of her tooth castle to stop hordes of bacteria from swarming up the walls to destroy her.

"Bombs away!" she yelled. "Isn't this super fun!" Her castle was made from teeth – from all of the teeth from all of the mouths from all of the children from all over the world. But years of attack from the barbarian bacteria had left the castle weak and riddled with decay. The teeth were rotting. They were as fragile as paper bricks. It was only a matter of time before the bacteria battered down her castle walls, stepped through the holes and helped themselves to her crown. If the tooth fairy was not to be overrun by the enemy she needed to rebuild her castle with good, solid teeth, but good, solid teeth were hard to find, because good, solid teeth did not fall out. Good, solid teeth were the ones in the gums!

"I have an idea," said the gum goblin, who was Head of Intelligence at the tooth fairy's HQ. If a tooth fell out in Guatemala, he heard it first. "Do you remember that small boy you visited last night?"

"Baby?" trilled the flighty young tooth fairy, who was easily distracted and relied on her advisers to keep her pointing in the right direction.

"Yes," replied the gum goblin, striding over to a tape recorder on his desk. "I recorded this conversation not thirty seconds ago." He pressed a button on the recorder and Girl's voice came over loud and clear.

"Grow up. She doesn't exist. That's Ma and Pa that is. They put that money under your pillow. . . Your childhood stops here. The tooth fairy's dead!"

"Tch! That really gets my goat!" puffed the tongue toad, a judicious toad with a handsomely long tongue that whispered words of wisdom in the tooth fairy's ear. "I can't stand it when children don't believe."

"What do you think we should do?" The tooth fairy's voice was full of excitement. "We could turn Girl's hair into a puffball and blow it to the four winds, or maybe I should dance her ragged? Oh, why don't I dance more often, dear Gummy, I do so love a gavotte or a cha-cha-cha!"

"We should teach her a lesson," declared the tongue toad, "and at the same time solve the tooth decay problem."

The gum goblin gasped. "Are you suggesting what I think you're suggesting?"

"Why, yes," said the toad, "I think I am."

"Well, isn't anyone going to tell *me*?" squealed the tooth fairy. "Why am I always the last to know anything around here?"

The tongue toad smiled broadly. "I'm intrigued," he said. "Does the word *pliers* mean anything to you?"

When Girl climbed into bed later that night, Baby was still crying downstairs. He'd been crying all day. It had come as a big shock to find that the tooth fairy did not exist. Girl heard the back door open and close, and from the silence she could tell that Ma and Pa had shut Baby out for the night, in the kennel in the garden. How much more peaceful life was without Baby! Her head touched the pillow, her mouth dropped open slightly and she fell asleep.

She was woken by the throbbing in her lip. She couldn't see what was going on, but it felt like someone had just punched her in the mouth. She tried to speak but her jaws wouldn't shut. She sat bolt upright.

"Watch out!" came a scream from inside her mouth. "Make a sudden move like that again and I'll have your tonsils out by mistake." Girl turned her head sideways and looked in the mirror. There was a metal clamp wedged into her mouth, holding her jaws open. Her chin was covered in blood, and inside her mouth she could see two coral-pink wings which shimmered when they caught the light.

"Whoever you are," she mumbled. "Get out of my mouth! Ow!" There was that stabbing pain again, like a cocktail stick jabbed into her gum. It was giving her a headache.

"Not long now," shouted the voice inside Girl's mouth. Only another sixteen to go!" And as the shrill little voice piped up in the dark, a white tooth flew out of Girl's mouth and landed on the eiderdown.

"Oy!" she shouted as best she could. "That's my tooth!"

"I know," said the tooth fairy, fluttering briefly on to Girl's bottom lip and skipping up on to the end of her nose. "I'm taking the lot if you don't mind, to refurbish the castle. Sorry about your fat lip by the way, I had to kick it open!"

"You're the tooth fairy!" gasped Girl.

"And you're a naughty girl for not believing in me," smiled the fairy. "Now if you'll excuse me I'd better get started on those big molars." She put away the pliers and produced a tiny pneumatic drill from behind her back. "I think they might prove a little tricky!" At which Girl passed clean out, and the tooth fairy jumped back into the gaping black hole to complete her night's work.

The next morning Girl was toothless, but when she showed Ma and Pa they just laughed, and when she asked if they'd buy her some dentures they laughed even louder. Girl was furious.

"I'll get even with that wicked tooth fairy if it's the last thing I do!" she muttered to herself.

"So the tooth fairy *does* exist!" yelped Baby jumping up outside the window like a dog. Which gave Girl an idea.

She ran down to the butchers and bought a bone. Then she ran along to the builder's yard and dipped the bone in concrete. Then she ran to the local park and threw the bone to an old dog with grey ears. No dog can resist a bone and this dog was no exception. When it took its first bite there was a terrible crack, a pained yelp and Girl pounced with a cunning glint in her eye.

As Girl slipped the dog's tooth under her pillow, the gum goblin felt a twitch in his ear.

"Tooth at the Pinchguts!" he said. "Under Girl's pillow."

"I thought we removed all her teeth last night," said the tongue toad.

"You do your job, I'll do mine," said the gum goblin tersely. "I heard a tooth. That's all there is to it."

"But what if it's a trap?"

"How can a tooth be a trap? A mouth is a trap, a tooth is a tooth!"

"All right, but don't say I didn't warn you."

"I never said that. Did I say that?" But the argument had long since become irrelevant, because the tooth fairy had already left for

Girl's house. Over the newly white-toothed castle wall she flew, over the field of deadly bacteria hiding in their filthy trenches, until she came to Girl's house, to the window that was normally closed, but on this particular occasion was *conveniently* open.

The tongue toad was right. It *was* a trap. As the tooth fairy rummaged under Girl's pillow, Girl snapped open her eyes and caught her like a butterfly.

"Gotcha!" she said. "Now here's what I want you to do."

"Let me go," screamed the coral-pink fairy. "You're wrinkling my wings!" But Girl wasn't letting go until the fairy had met her demands.

"Take me home to your castle and give me back my teeth," she whistled, picking up a slipper. "Or I'll squash you with this and ruin toothless nights for children all over the world!"

"But you don't understand," the fairy trembled. "Your teeth are the only good teeth

I've got. I used them to rebuild my castle wall. If I give them back my castle will be devoured by bacteria!"

"Oh dear," smiled Girl heartlessly. She squeezed harder. "Looks like you can't win either way."

The tooth fairy did not like the look of that slipper. She took Girl's hand and flew her back to her castle, where the gum goblin and tongue toad were waiting to greet her.

"You will fetch my good, strong teeth now!" she ordered.

"Only if you promise not to be such a spoilsport in future," replied the gum goblin.

"No deals," roared Girl, raising her slipper. "One false move and the tooth fairy gets it!"

"So you admit that the tooth fairy does exist?"

"Teeth!" bellowed Girl. "While *you*," she said pointing to the tongue toad, "will stand by to hop me home the moment I'm fully toothed up again!"

"I really must protest," interrupted the tongue toad. "This is not a good idea. The wall was built to keep the evil bacteria out. If we pull it down we'll be ransacked!"

But his protests came too late, because just then the gum goblin arrived with a sack that was full of Girl's good, strong teeth that he'd pulled from the castle wall. He presented them to her and held up a mirror while she popped them back in. But the moment she had she wished she hadn't. She had just climbed aboard the toad when a fearful slurping shook the castle to its roots. The enamel wall was breached.

The bacteria swarmed into the castle and slimed over the bridge into the Crown Chamber.

"What do you want?" asked the tooth fairy with dignity.

"Teeth!" grunted their leader, a brute of an organism called Bacillus Maximus. "We eat good teeth! Give us one mouthful of good teeth and we'll go away!"

But the gum goblin didn't have any, the tongue toad didn't have any and the tooth fairy had lost hers years before, in a fight over a hand of poker.

Which just left Girl. Before she could close her mouth, Bacillus Maximus spotted the tell-tale white gleam and with a loud blast of his whistle he waved his troops forward. Girl realized that she was in a spot of bother and tried to pull her teeth out again, but they were stuck fast. She tried to run, but a legion of germs blocked her way. Like a swarm of black flies they overwhelmed her. She tried to scream but her teeth had turned to goo in her mouth, and in less than a minute the bacteria had gone and Girl was just a puddle of smelly, brown sludge.

Which meant that the Pinchguts were able to bury her in a cheap fizzy-pop bottle instead of an expensive brass-handled coffin. And that, as Ma and Pa told Baby, "was something of a result!" And when Baby lost his next tooth he pretended to be asleep until the tooth fairy was actually underneath his pillow dragging the tooth out. When she re-emerged he had his eyes open.

"Hello," he grinned excitedly. "I knew Girl was wrong." The tooth fairy heaved the tooth into the rucksack on her back and prepared for take off. "I knew you existed."

"I knew I existed too," she winked. Then she fluttered out into the night sky and headed for home with Baby's voice booming behind her.

"Give my love to Father Christmas, the Easter Bunny, the baby stork, the little leprechauns and the Yeti!"

So she did.

Dirty Bertie

PARENT WARNING!
This tale contains filthy, dirty language.
Please ensure that your sensitive and
shockable parents are fully protected.
Make them wear ear-plugs!

Mr and Mrs Barf used to laugh about their name sounding like "bath". No one else ever found this funny, but they did, because they were two of the cleanest people on the planet, taking three baths a day. They kept a neat and tidy house as well, with labels and rotas and sofas covered in wipe-down plastic to ward off dust.

"Dirt is the devil," Mrs Barf had informed her husband on their wedding night. "Cleanliness is next to godliness, husband, and let us pray that we never forget it."

They were Christian, God-fearing folk who believed that polishing and dusting got you a backstage pass into heaven.

Imagine their horror then, when their only son Bertie turned out to be a juvenile hobo – a grimy, filthy, unwashed, dirt magnet whose hatred of water exceeded that of a cat-in-a-sack's. They wanted a child who scrubbed up well for church; whose skin shone like a polished apple; whose ears squeaked; whose nails gleamed; whose teeth sparkled, and whose clean clothes smelt as sweet as butterscotch clouds in a munchmallow sky. What they actually got was a slurry pit on legs, dry, empty baths and moth-eaten flannels. Bertie was dirty. Soap was his sworn enemy; shampoo was witch spit; toothpaste was squeezed from the slime hole of a slug – or so Bertie thought. His toothbrush was only ever used to scrape squashed worms off the soles of his trainers. His hairbrush was never used at all. It gathered dust under his bed until six orphaned hedgehogs stole it in the mistaken belief that it was their dead mother. As a result, his hair looked like a fur-ball that a cat had coughed up. The insides of his ears looked like last year's guacamole – green and crusty, and certainly not something you'd dip a corn chip in. His fingernails were as black as a peat bog. His top lip was covered in a flaky crust of hardened nose-drip. A selection of winter vegetables blossomed in the compost behind his ears. His armpits were long overdue a visit from Rentokil, and his feet were slimier than a bucket of buttered tadpoles.

As for his clothes, they never went near the washing machine, and bear in mind that this was a boy to whom food *stuck*! Chocolate chips, tomato ketchup, sausage skins, jam, anchovies, raisins, milkshake, ratatouille, peanut butter, fruit pie, stilton and ice cream all played their part in creating the psychedelic design down the front of his T-shirt and jeans. He looked like a hippie and smelled like a goat.

Stink clouds followed him down the street, curling the corners of paving slabs like old sandwiches, wilting lampposts and dissolving queues in the twitch of a nose.

One thing Dirty Bertie had no problem getting hold of was a hot fish supper, because whenever he entered the fish and chip shop every other customer left.

Getting dirty was not a problem for Bertie. Like most boys, he was born with the skill already in him, but *staying* dirty required consummate professionalism. To avoid the use of the "cursed water", Bertie invented diseases that could only be cured by prolonged dryness – scaly hands, floaty feet, sponge liver, rusty kidneys, freeze dried belly button (which, when wet, swelled to twelve times its normal size, apparently) duck phobia and heavy brain, which was caused by an over-saturation of rainwater. But on the one day when his parents refused to listen to his excuses – "If you grow shoots out the soles of your feet, Bertie, we'll plant you in the garden, that's all there is to it!" – Bertie did what any normal boy would do when confronted with a bath he didn't want. He rang the council and told them he'd just been rushed by a huge, plague-carrying rat. The bathroom was then closed and sixteen workmen arrived to search for Bertie's lie. And, of course, while sixteen workmen were standing around shaking their heads and drinking tea, nobody could get into the bathroom, let alone take a bath!

"Please have a bath," pleaded his father, one day. He'd just been handing out clothes-pegs to their niffed-off neighbours. "If you do, Bertie, you can walk on the carpet and sit on the sofa. How's that for a treat?"

"I can't bathe today," replied his smutty son.

"Why not?" wailed his mother. "Why does water give you the willies?"

"Rabies!" shrieked his father, out of the blue. "It's classic. The boy has aquaphobia – a fear of water, brought on by rabies!"

"I have a fear of drowning my pets," corrected Bertie.

"Pets?"

Dirty Bertie laid his wild mop of hair on the kitchen table and shook his head. A cloud of insects rose from the tangled strands like birds in a cornfield frightened by gunshot. Fleas and lice were followed out of the bush by a family of ladybirds, two kissing stag beetles, a snail, a nesting housemartin with a twig in its beak, three worms, an old tramp's shoe, a pedal and a startled mouse with a towel round its waist. Bertie's mother leapt on to her chair and shrieked, while his father tucked his trousers into his socks to foil any insect infestation.

That night, having protected themselves with deep-sea diving suits and breathing equipment, his parents attempted to steal his niff-stiff clothes with extendable tongs, but Bertie had rigged up a sophisticated trip-wire, floodlight and klaxon system, which caught them red-handed. The next day, they hired a crop duster to spray the garden with disinfectant while Bertie took his afternoon snooze in the compost heap, but the pilot got his wings wedged between two houses. So they swapped his mattress for a sheep-dip tank and hid it under his duvet, hoping that he wouldn't notice when he jumped into bed. But they left a sheep in by mistake and her bleating gave the game away. The day after that, they threw out the telly and informed Bertie that from now on the family would be making its own entertainment, like people did in olden days.

"I've got a parlour game from the Middle Ages!" cried his mother. "One of us sits in these stocks," (she produced some from behind her back), "while the other two throw wet sponges at him. Bertie, why don't you start?" But Bertie could spot an attempted sponge bath at fifty paces and sat in the chimney till the sponges were destroyed.

Despairingly, Mr Barf hired a wallpaper stripper, pretended to trip on a radish and *accidentally* tried to steam-strip his own son. It didn't work. Bertie ducked to one side and his father stripped the dog instead. The Yorkshire terrier was never the same dog again. It looked like a pink chihuahua.

*

Mrs Barf had reached the end of her tether. "If God had meant us to be dirty he wouldn't have given us washable skins," she told Bertie.

"He should have made us out of plastic then," he replied. "He should have covered us in anoraks all over."

The housemartin flapped out of his hair and flew off for worms.

"Oh Bertie, think of your future," urged his mother. "People won't give you a job if you're dirty."

"Rubbish," he scoffed. "There are plenty of jobs for dirty people."

"Really?" said his father. "I'd be interested to hear what they are."

Bertie hadn't thought. "Erm . . . farmers."

His father shook his head. "I'm afraid not. Farmers' wives always make them take a bath."

"Coal miners, then?"

"Not coal miners either. Pit bosses always make them shower with the ponies."

"All right," said Bertie defiantly. "Footballers. Footballers get dirty."

"Some do," smiled his father smugly, "but

they've all got rich rock-star girlfriends who make them scrub up in tubs of champagne."

"You see," said his mother triumphantly. "Nobody likes a dirty Bertie! If you want to get on in this world, you have to be clean." Bertie grinned slyly. A brainwave had occurred.

"Not if you're an astronaut!" he said. It was a masterstroke of quick thinking, and by the look on his parents' faces Bertie knew that he'd out-boxed them. "Astronauts aren't clean, mother. Did you know," he sniggered (in that dirty way that boys do, when they wrinkle their noses like pug-dogs with colds), "astronauts don't even take their suits off when they go to the loo!"

"You don't really want to be an astronaut!" shrieked his father.

"I do," said Bertie, now digging his heels in. "I've always wanted to fly rockets into space; I've always wanted to zap and beam and star-date my log; and I've always wanted to vaporize bug-eyed monsters with purple lump-guns. Astronauting's my ideal job. In fact, I've heard that unless you smell like a dead badger, they won't let you in."

And with that, Dirty Bertie, his mind now tuned to matters Martian, unlocked the back door and went outside to build himself a space rocket.

He used the potting shed as a cockpit; a large plastic ice cream (stolen from the roof of an ice cream van and rammed through the shed roof) as a nose cone; and his mother's rotating washing line, next door's satellite dish and a police car's hub cap as communication antennae. He cut pictures of planets out of an expensive encyclopaedia and stuck them in the shed windows to give himself a realistic view. And he ran an extension cable from his parents' bedroom, and used their telephone as his link to mission control, which just happened to be a take-away pizza restaurant seconds down the road.

Meanwhile, indoors, while Dirty Bertie was blasting planets, saving alien princesses, liquidating robots, pulverizing pirates and scoffing pizzas in a parallel universe, his parents came up with a foolproof plan to break their son of his dirty habit.

"We'll find him a girlfriend," said his father. "If love doesn't smarten him up, nothing will."

Then they put an advert in the local paper and sat back to wait for the doorbell to ring.

Girlfriend wanted for church-going boy with loving parents. All candidates to turn up at 10 o'clock on Saturday morning for a gander at the goods.

At 9.45am the following Saturday, there was a familiar ring to the conversation.

"Why won't you let me tidy you up?" whined Bertie's mother.

"I'm an astronaut," said Bertie. "I follow the astronaut's creed. *Can't wash. Won't wash.*"

"But no girl's going to love you smelling like a dustcart."

"They will," whispered Mr Barf. "Love is blind, dear." He stared at her fly-away hair, her double chin and piggy eyes. "Remember?"

The first girl was wearing her party dress and flounced into the room in a flutter of frills and bows, but when she saw Bertie she screamed and ran out again.

The second girl had thick pebble glasses and a glistening brace on her teeth. When *she* saw Bertie she smiled. This time it was Bertie who screamed and ran out.

The third girl took one look at the cloud of flies that buzzed around Bertie's dirty hair and fell to the floor in a dead faint. On her way home, she told the paramedic in the ambulance that she thought the boy was dead.

The fourth girl never made it through the door. She hated gerbils, and that's what she thought she could smell.

The fifth girl saw the fourth girl being sick in a hedge and didn't come in, and the sixth girl. . . . Well, the sixth girl wasn't a girl. Come to think of it, it wasn't a boy either.

Bertie opened the front door (his parents were too busy spraying the sitting room with air freshener) and discovered to his astonishment that the person ringing the bell was none other than HIMSELF! His jaw must have hit the front step, because the lookalike laughed.

"Sorry," it said. "Thoughtless, I know, but I had to borrow someone's body in a rush and I saw yours through the window."

"Who are you?" goldfished Bertie.

"Can't stand out here chatting," said the all-too-familiar stranger pushing his way in and shutting the door. "They're out there now. They were just behind me. Trying to find a hover spot for their spacewagon."

"Are you an escaped lunatic?" asked Bertie.

"I'm a chameleon," came the reply. "From Tharg. Name's Pyg." He extended an arm which mutated as Bertie went to shake it. As the bones in the creature's face stretched and twisted into an altogether lumpier configuration, the arm turned green like a giant squid's tentacle. Gone was Bertie's mirror image. In its place stood PygAlien, half reptile, half kangaroo, half deep-sea blob. Bertie could not take it all in.

"Tharg," he stumbled. "That's in . . . er. . ." Where was Tharg? ". . .in Scotland, right?"

"In the Fourteenth Astral Belt of Zimeon. I thought every astronaut knew that."

"Sorry," gasped Bertie. "Astronaut?"

"You are an astronaut, aren't you? I mean you're certainly dirty enough to be one. You *smell* like one." That was the nicest thing anyone had ever said to Bertie. "And that is your space rocket in the garden."

"No, that's not real."

"Of course it's real. That's why I'm here."

"No. It's a shed."

"Mine crashed. I have to borrow yours to get home in a hurry."

"But I'm not an astronaut," protested Bertie for the last time. "I'm just Dirty Bertie. And my dad'll kill me if you take his shed." PygAlien tapped a small flashing watch on his wrist.

"They're here," he said, slapping a weapon that looked like a whisk into Bertie's hand. "Only use that if you have to. Let's go."

"Go?! Where?! What is this?!"

While they ran to Bertie's space rocket, or rather while Bertie ran and the alien glooped, leaving puddles of slime in its wake, PygAlien told Bertie why he was being chased.

"Disco fever," he said. "Complete misunderstanding. I was at a disco in Tharg. It was dark. I snogged completely the wrong girl. When the lights came back on, I discovered that the object of my passion was nine hundred and forty years old. She had a face like a bag of spanners and she was rotting. Her arm came off in my hand." But Bertie wasn't listening.

"I'm not an astronaut," he said. "Being dirty, that's just who I am. I'm Dirty Bertie."

PygAlien hauled open the shed door and surveyed the cockpit, which comprised two garden forks, an upturned hover-mower and a deckchair set to face the muddy window.

"God preserve us!" groaned Pyg, picking up a plant pot. "Put this helmet on. When we put this old tub through its paces, things may get a bit bumpy."

"But sheds don't fly," pleaded Bertie as the alien rammed the flowerpot over his ears.

"So anyway," it continued, "I told this rotten hag – Putrid, her name was – that I never wanted to see her again. Unfortunately she screamed and said that I was just like all the others. That was when her two brothers appeared and told me I'd offended their family. Turns out they're space mafia. Fingers in every pie in the sky. Now I've got a choice – marry the dog or die. That's why you've got to fly me out of here!"

"But I'm not an astronaut," whimpered Bertie. "And this is a shed."

Back indoors, having freshened the sitting-room air to their satisfaction, Bertie's parents had just stepped into the hall when the front door burst off its hinges and pinned them to the floor.

"Where is he?" slurped the ugly old crone at the front door. Spit drooled from the corners of her mouth as she scratched an itch under her wig and sneezed. Her nose flew off across the hall and landed on a coat peg, nostril down. Her elephantine skin flapped off her shrunken bones like wrinkled curtains. Her body stank of rotting fish and cheap scent. Her face was caked in make-up. It was Putrid, and by her side were two large walruses wearing dark glasses and suits.

"Where's the ignition switch?" screamed PygAlien.

"It doesn't have one." said Bertie.

"Every rocket's got an ignition switch!"

"This is a shed," blubbed the boy. "I'm not an astronaut."

"How about a key?" asked the anxious alien. "If we don't blast off now, there's no saying what those two brothers will do to us when they get here."

"US!" squealed Bertie. "But I never kissed anyone."

"Come on, who are you trying to kid!" roared the alien, slapping Bertie across the back. "Any astronaut who smells as bad and looks as dirty as you do has got to have done his fair share of kissing." Suddenly Bertie didn't want to be dirty any more. He was giving the wrong impression. But that was nothing to the impression he was about to give.

*

When the shed door banged open, PygAlien and Bertie were looking the other way, but they knew who it was. They could smell her. They swung round and saw, framed in the doorway between two henchmen, the silhouette of a two-metre Walnut Whip. It was only when Putrid shuffled forward, and the light from the window fell across her face, that Bertie got an eyeful of the full horror. Her skin was flapping off in strips. Cream-coloured bone was clearly visible, and through the hole where her nose had been, he could see daylight. She had wooden teeth that clacked in her mouth, and limbs that were either nailed to her body or stuck back on with sticking plaster. Her clothes were shredded, her eyeballs kept popping out of their sockets, and a constant stream of goo dripped from a hole in her neck and dribbled to the floor. She was, without doubt, the ugliest, most repulsive, most sickening specimen that Bertie had ever seen. She quite liked *him*, though.

"I'm sorry," whimpered PygAlien as Putrid and her brothers stepped forward. "I didn't mean to upset you."

"Shut it!" growled one of the brothers. "Do we take him?"

"No," commanded his slurrified sister. "Why would I marry *him*," she pointed at PygAlien, "when I could have *him*!" Her finger moved across the shed and picked out Bertie. "Yum-yum," she slurped. "He's a dreamboat!"

"A dreamboat!" Bertie flew into a blind panic. "No, I'm not. Stay away!" He pointed the whisk at the mafia. "Do you have any idea what this thing can do?"

"Whisk eggs?" giggled Putrid, whipping the kitchen utensil out of his hand. "Oh, do stop playing hard to get."

"But I'm not a dreamboat. I'm Dirty Bertie. I smell like a warthog."

"Yes, you do, don't you! You're deliciously dirty," said the monstrous crone, fluttering her eyelids so fast that they flew off the front of her face. "You smell like a scrummy cesspit!" Her thick yellow tongue licked her greasy, grey lips with a salacious slurp. "Boys, I think I'm in heaven. I'm in love and I've changed my mind." Bertie's eyes stuck out like organ stops.

"No, don't say it!" he cried. But she did.

"Take Dirty Bertie instead!"

It was a foul piece of luck. If Bertie hadn't been dirty, the alien-love-Nan would never have fancied him. If he hadn't stunk like a skunk she'd have taken PygAlien instead. But as it was, the Walrus brothers kidnapped Dirty Bertie and took him back to Tharg to marry Putrid, and that is where he remains to this day – still as dirty as ever. The only difference now is that Bertie would *willingly* take a bath, if it would stop his wife Putrid from kissing him.

Back at home, Mr and Mrs Barf found an alien in the garden shed.

"Where's Bertie?" shrieked Mrs Barf.

"Upstairs taking a bath," lied PygAlien. "I'll just go and get him."

And when Bertie stepped out of the bathroom five minutes later, he was as clean as a shiny new whistle. And from that day on Mr and Mrs Barf and the chameleon from Tharg lived happily ever after.

The People Potter

The legend goes something like this. It was 1777. Mr Josiah Reeks was a potter, the Master Figure-maker at the world-famous Worcester pottery, a solitary, silent man who shunned the company of others and spent his life hunched over a potter's wheel in pursuit of perfection.

Then one fateful day, a group of children kicked their pig's bladder through the window of the pottery's stock room. The bladder smashed several precious porcelain china figures, and the children, in their clumsy attempts to retrieve their ball, smashed many more. Unfortunately, it was Josiah Reeks who stumbled across this scene of destruction. Unfortunately, it was *his* life's work that lay ruined on the floor. Unfortunately, the children had not escaped by the time he locked the door. Or so the legend goes. And when he re-emerged three days later, covered in dust and clay, there were twelve new figures in the store room – twelve life-size porcelain figures – all children, all with a glazed, faraway look in their eyes. They were potteryfied.

They say that Josiah Reeks went into the stock room sane, but came out as mad as blue biscuits. They say that he was bricked up in a tiny, hot cell and died from the stifling heat as if toasted in a kiln. They say that for two hundred years his ghost has potteryfied clumsy children all over the world. They say that you know when he's after you, because of the lingering smell of wet clay and the swish-swirling sound of his potter's wheel. They say that he's called the People Potter. But who's to say that *they* are right?

Greta Gawky was a clumsy girl. She was nearly

two metres tall and was still only ten. Her long arms and legs had a life of their own and flailed around her body like the tentacles of a sky-diving octopus. When she walked into a classroom at school, the other children would cry, "Lawks, it's Gawks!" and would dive under their desks and cover their heads in case she knocked the blackboard off the wall, or slipped on a piece of chalk and flattened them with her whirling satchel as she windmilled through the window. In her time she had done both. For Greta, achieving the simplest of tasks was impossible without wholesale destruction of her immediate surroundings. When she went fishing with her father, she cast her hook through the car window, yanked off the handbrake and sent the car rolling into the river. When she mailed a please-tell-me-how-to-be-a-dainty-daffodil letter to the magazine, *Clumsy Lummocks*, she got her hand stuck in the post box. When she went shopping, she fell into the ice-cream freezer and had to be pulled out by the Kingcones. She just didn't think. She saw what she wanted and went for it.

"Hello, little dog," she said, bending down to pat the nervous Pekinese on the head, but it was less of a pat and more of a blow, and the little dog flew ten metres up a tree, left its elderly owner dangling off a branch and caused a stampede of squirrels through a sock shop. "It wasn't my fault!" she protested. It never was. "It was an accident!" Wrong again.

She needed to leave things alone. She needed to stop prodding and pushing and nosing around like a rat in a sewer. She needed to look not touch, to think before she acted, to put her brain into gear before she lifted a finger. But clumsy people never do.

At home in Worcester, her poor parents lived in constant terror of what she'd break next. And they had good reason. In the hall, just behind the wellington boots, was the family nest egg – a Ming vase worth half a million pounds. Mr Gawky had found it in a skip. From the day she was born, it was made clear to clumsy Greta that she should never ever touch this vase, and as a result she grew up wondering if a magic genie lived inside.

When she was nine, her curiosity got the better of her and she tried to climb inside with a plate of toast for the genie's breakfast, but the vase toppled over. Had it not been for the fact that the sleeping dog broke the vase's fall (as well as two of its own ribs) it would surely have smashed.

"It wasn't me," Greta lied to her parents. "It couldn't be me. You told me not to touch it." But *they* knew. *Everyone* knew.

That night, her parents smeared the vase with butter to stop their daughter getting a grip. Greta was so intent on seeing this genie, however, that she rigged up a hand mirror on a piece of string, stood on the landing and lowered it gently into the neck of the vase to see what she could see. Unfortunately it was too dark to see anything, so she lowered a lit candle on a piece of string, but the flame burnt through the string, the lit candle fell into the vase, the vase heated up, the butter melted and it cost £75 to have the carpet cleaned.

"How could it possibly be my fault?" whined Greta, trying to argue the unarguable. "I was upstairs when the butter melted!"

The next day, her parents caged their precious china vase in a padded wooden crate, which they stupidly thought would protect it for ever. What they hadn't bargained on was Greta's shoelace working itself loose in the kitchen. When the ham-fisted girl bent down to tie it up again, she nudged the gas tap on the hob with her bottom, hit the ignition switch with her hand and torched the crate to a cinder. "How was I to know you cooked on a flame-thrower?" she protested.

The next day, the vase was hoisted off the ground in a cargo net. For a short while mid-air suspension seemed the perfect solution, until Greta decided to dance the Dance of the Sugar-Plum Fairy while waiting for her bath to run. She had just pirouetted on to the loo seat when the water overflowed. As she executed a heavy *pas de chat*, she, and four hundred litres of water, crashed through the ceiling like a waterfall. It took six firemen and one tub of axle grease to slide Greta out of the neck of the Ming vase, which had been *very* dark inside and sadly lacking a genie.

After the flood, her parents decided that they could not afford to take any more chances. So they lied to her. "If you break the Ming vase," her mother said sweetly, "we will all be ruined. Your father and I will be shipped off to a slave market in Marrakesh, and you will be sent to a big house on Clapham Common to start work as a celery maid."

Greta's eyes nearly popped out of her head "Is that like a scullery maid," she gasped, "who polishes skulls in a dungeon?"

"No," lied her mother for a second time. "A celery maid is made to eat celery every meal for the rest of her life."

"Oh yuck!" spat the girl, "I hate celery!" She ran around in circles to get the bad taste out of her mouth and knocked a paperweight off the bureau. It fell with a sickening splat on to the little house in the gerbil's cage.

"Leave it!" winced her mother. "We'll scrape that up later!"

But the Marrakesh-celery lie had its effect. From that day on, Greta always took the greatest of care when she was in the presence of the precious Ming vase. Apart from that silly game of indoor golf, that trivial incident with the runaway motor mower, and that memorable attempt to fly a kite in the hall with a hair-dryer, the vase was never in danger again!

Then, one Friday evening, a parcel arrived for Greta. It was marked THIS WAY UP – BREAKABLE. Her excited parents hopped around behind her chair and urged her to open it.

"Do you know what it is?" Greta asked, as her fingers slipped off the knot and catapulted the spoon out of the mustard, splattering her father's wine with fiery, yellow globs. She was quick to shift the blame. "Your fault for leaving the spoon in the jar," she said.

"Just open the present," sighed her father, drinking his mustard wine and pulling a sour face.

"We found it in an antique shop," her mother explained, as Greta peeled off the paper and revealed a faded green box. "The man in the shop said it would encourage you to take more care."

"What's that noise?" said Greta suddenly, turning round to check the room. She couldn't pin down where it was coming from. "It's a sort of whirring noise. Spinning, whooshing, swishing. There! Listen!" But her parents could hear nothing. It was like a freewheeling bicycle, Greta thought, or someone sweeping leaves off a path. And there was a funny smell too. What was it? Mud?

"Open your present, Greta." Her father's voice sounded weary as he tugged his dreamy daughter back into the real world.

When she removed the lid of the box she found a tiny porcelain figure lying on a quilt of white tissue paper. "It's Worcester," said her mother. "1795. Over two hundred years old. Do you like it?" Greta wasn't sure. It was a figure of a grey-haired man with jug ears, a pinched mouth, a receding chin and a long nose that made him look like a china teapot. He was wearing a rather drab frock coat and was carrying under his arm a round silver tray.

"Is he a waiter?" queried Greta.

"No," smirked her father. "Look what he's

standing on." It was a small hill made from lumps of clay, broken china and children's toys. Greta didn't understand. "That's not a tray, Greta, that's a potter's wheel." Still nothing. "He's The People Potter."

"Ohhhh," said Greta as if she finally understood. "Who's he?"

Greta's parents told her the legend of the pig's bladder and she listened with open ears.

"But why did he potteryfy the children?" she asked.

"To teach them a lesson," said her father. "They were clumsy and china breaks."

"Oh," said Greta, warily eyeing the porcelain figure. "I've never seen anything like it."

"That's because it's the only one in the whole world," said her mother.

"Why didn't they make more?"

"Because it wasn't made. It just appeared in the Worcester factory one day. Look." Her father took the figurine out of the box and turned it upside down. On the base there was a crude poem.

Do not break me. Pass me on
To a clumsy minor.
Let them know that if I smash
I'm coming back from China.

"What does *that* mean?" Greta gasped.

"Nobody's quite sure," said her mother. "But the man in the shop said that you should look after it and under no circumstances let it smash."

"Or what?"

"Or the People Potter will come back from China!" Her mother and father roared with laughter. "We don't know, Greta. Stop looking so serious. It's only a bit of nonsense. We thought it might make you more careful, that's all."

"Got you," said Greta. "Thanks."

Far from making her more careful, however, the presence of the porcelain People Potter made Greta more and more nervous, and the worst thing you can do to a clumsy person is to make them nervous, because nerves are to clumsiness what fire-lighters are to barbecues. Instead of becoming *less* clumsy, she became *more* clumsy. She stood up to get the milk from the fridge, forgetting that she'd tucked the tablecloth into her collar, because she didn't have a napkin.

"Whoops!" She cleared the table in one clean sweep, stippling the walls with marmalade, filling the lampshade with tea and creating a sandy-beach effect on the floor with the sugar. She took one look at the ugly, glowering porcelain figure on the kitchen table and ran wailing from the room. As she screeched into the hall, however, she caught her cardigan on the door handle and tore off a button. But she wasn't stopping for anything. Not even the swish-swirling noise in her head. She raced upstairs, broke three stair rods with her thumping feet, unravelled a wrinkle of stair-carpet and dived into her bedroom.

Her parents took one look at the mess in the kitchen, took one look at each other and shouted.

"Greta! We're going out! We'll be back in

two hours, by which time we expect you to have tidied up the house." Then they stroked their beloved Ming vase and left, shutting the door behind them. As they did so, Greta's button rolled across the hallway, bumped into the fifteenth-century vase and spun to a standstill on the floor.

Through cold, glassy eyes, the porcelain figure of the People Potter saw it all.

Greta stood up from her bed and wiped her runny nose with the corner of her cardigan. That was when she noticed the missing button. Horror! Her grandmother had knitted that cardigan and was visiting tomorrow. The People Potter was slung from her mind. The button had to be found! She dashed out of her room and switched off the light as she went. What she didn't know was that her flood of nervous tears had collected in a puddle on the floor, and that the puddle had dripped through the boards on to a frayed electrical wire. When she flicked the light switch, the wires shorted out and a spark set fire to her rug.

Meanwhile, galloping down the stairs, Greta

was doing her usual trick of not looking where she was going. Her foot slipped on the loose carpet that she'd rucked up minutes before, and her legs shot out either side of the banisters. "Aah! Ooh! Aah! Ooh! Aah!" She bumped down the stairs on her bottom, snapping posts in half, and spraying splinters to either side like a snow-plough clearing snow. She hit the newel post at speed, uprooted it from the floor and somersaulted on to the lampshade hanging from the hall ceiling. The light was not designed to take her weight. The flex snapped and Greta crashed through the hall floor into the cellar, where she accidentally fell on top of the pipe that pumped mains water into the house.

With a rumble and roar a water fountain burst through the fracture, and Greta shot up in the air like a beach ball on a geyser, straight back through the hole she'd just made in the floor, and up through the ceiling into the bathroom. As she passed through the hall she caught a glimpse of the Ming vase sitting precariously in the middle of this devastation.

She squeaked as if a little squirrel had just punched her in the stomach. She had to save the vase!

She grabbed on to the bath taps and tried to pull herself down off the water spout, but the pipes that fed these taps ran up towards the tank in the loft and she pulled with such force that the pipes ripped out of the wall, the ceiling collapsed and the contents of the loft crashed down into the bath. No bath is designed to support that much weight. With a shuddering clang, it plummeted into the hall, bounced off the hatstand and crashed through the wall into the sitting room. It came to a halt with its clawed feet wedged firmly in the torn sofa covers. Greta had hitched a ride, and now she climbed out across the coffee table, which collapsed under her weight and fired a bowl of flowers at the CD player, which fell to the ground and switched itself on (playing that old-time classic "Fly Me To The Moon").

Greta crawled into the hall to check on the Ming vase, but – and this is where it starts to get bizarre – it was at that precise moment that the fire in her bedroom set off the fire alarm. This had three effects: 1) The high-pitched wailing increased Greta's sense of panic. 2) A neighbour heard the noise and called the fire brigade. 3) The driver of the "Mole" – which was a huge drilling machine that Worcester City Council was using to dig Worcester's first underground railway system – heard what he thought was the lunch-break siren and, hungry for his cheese and pickle sandwich, he started to turn his machine around. Only that was also when the steering wheel locked and the throttle jammed. "It can't happen!" the manufacturers told the council when they bought the drill, but it had. The driver jumped ship and left the runaway Mole drilling upwards at one metre per second. And, as you've probably guessed, the only object between it and heaven was Greta's house.

Greta was back in the hall, clambering over the rubble to reach the precious Ming vase, when she suddenly remembered the porcelain figure of the People Potter. Horror! She had to save that too! But, as she turned towards the kitchen, two hard jets of water knocked her off her feet. It was the Fire Brigade. And just as well they turned up when they did, because all of a sudden the Mole screeched through the cellar, the roof shuddered and the walls started to buckle and fold inwards like a house of cards!

As luck would have it, that was when the CD jammed and played the first five notes of "Fly Me To The Moon" in a loud repetitive cycle. Well, a spacecraft must have picked up the signal (as they do) and the alien captain must have thought it was another spacecraft in trouble. Whatever the reason, one moment Greta was in mortal danger, pinned to the ground by a man-mincing monster mole machine, the next she was safely suspended in a beam of light that was shining from the bottom of an alien space craft. Then, as the Mole churned its way harmlessly through the back garden, Greta was lowered into the rubble next to the Ming vase and the alien blasted back into space. Its rockets ignited with a mighty roar and blew the roof of Greta's house off.

Not that she noticed, because just then she found the missing button. And more importantly, there wasn't a scratch on it. Her grandmother would be pleased.

Suddenly the house groaned. It was a low, mournful sound, like a wild sea-wind whistling through rigging. It was the sound of wood being torn apart, of metal twisting, of nails pinging out of buckled joints. Then the house collapsed.

Greta was lucky to escape with her life. She was lucky to escape with the Ming vase intact too. When she opened her eyes only two things were left standing – the precious vase and the front door. There was a knock from the outside. But Greta did not answer. Her desperate eyes were searching for the porcelain figure of the People Potter. The kitchen table had been smashed into firewood. She couldn't see it! There was a second knock on the door. It was more impatient. Look, Greta, look! And then she saw it, lying behind a fallen beam in a thousand shattered pieces. She gasped with cold horror. What had the poem said?

Do not break me. Pass me on
To a clumsy minor.
Let them know that if I smash
I'm coming back from China.

The front door swung open of its own accord, shifting the debris behind it.

"It wasn't my fault. It was an accident!" cried Greta, gawping at the grey-haired man with a beaky face like a teapot.

"Who's a clumsy clod?" said the People Potter.

"Go away!" squeaked the girl, realizing at once what the poem meant. *Coming back from China* meant coming back from the dead! And this spook was not about to go away, not after he'd spent two hundred years waiting to arrive. Besides, he had work to do, which was why he'd brought his potter's wheel!

When Greta's parents returned home after their walk, their home had gone, and their clumsy daughter had been turned into a life-size porcelain figure with a glazed, faraway look in her eyes.

"She's been potteryfied by the People Potter!" gasped her mother. "How's the Ming vase?"

"Fine," said her catatonic father. "Not a scratch on it!"

Clumsy Greta was now as fragile as the Ming vase. She couldn't clump. She couldn't gawk. She couldn't lumber. In fact she couldn't even blink for fear of breaking herself. She became so quiet and careful that people often mistook her for a real statue.

Just remember; the potter's wheel is always spinning.

It's Only a Game, Sport!

This story was told to me by an old Australian bushman in an old Australian bar. After loosening his neck with six tubes of the amber nectar, this is how he told it.

G'day! Ever wondered why we Australians build our houses on stilts? And it's not to get the aerial higher for better reception on our television sets. I mean, what'd be the point? Have you seen the programmes they make us watch? God save us all from Australian soap operas! I'd rather watch a sheep pass a tapeworm! No, the reason we build our houses off the ground (so you've got to climb up a ladder to get to the front door) is snakes. You should see the size of some of our snakes! Make your hair curl, they would. Make your toes curl as well, if they bit you. Deadly, they are, the taipan, the copper head and the death adder. Never stop to ask the time of a taipan, because when you meet one of those poisonous fellas, it's time for one thing and one thing only – it's time to meet your maker!

Anyhow, that's snakes. This is a story about a bad loser. It's about a boy called Bruce, his mother Sheila, his father Shane and his little sister, Kitty. They lived in one of these houses on stilts, and kept a pet koala in the kitchen. When they were young, Shane and Sheila were pretty damned famous for being athletes. They were fit and tanned and both had long hair, bleached blonde by the sun. When they got older, they fell apart a bit, but that's a different story. In their prime, Sheila and Shane were top dogs at all sports – running, cricket, swimming, football, rugby, tennis, crocodile wrestling, kangaroo boxing, scorpion scrapping . . . you name it, they won it. But all this success went to their heads and the idea that one could play a game for fun soon became an alien concept to them. They *only* played to win.

Now the trouble with parents is that they assume that what was right for them must also be right for their kids. When their son, Bruce, was born, both of them assumed that he'd be a chip off the old block, so they taught him that winning was everything and that losing was not an option. And lo and behold, Bruce became a nightmare in nappies! He had to win everything! From sandcastle-building to Pik-a-Stik, from platypus-riding to Snap, from cheese-rolling to Hangman, from wombat racing to Draw The Well Dry – whatever it was, Bruce had to be best! He had to destroy the other runners in the egg and spoon race, humiliate the creepers in Grandmother's Footsteps, and eat every child in the room in What's The Time, Mr Wolf? But of course he *didn't*, because he *wasn't* a chip off the old block. Life had dealt Bruce an ironic hand. How shall I put this? He was bad at games. He was basically uncoordinated. He was the boy whose boot came off when he kicked the ball; the boy who let go of the cricket bat in the middle of the shot; the boy who tripped over his own feet; the boy with the pigeon chest and the matchstick arms and legs.

It was because of this, and because he had to win at everything but couldn't, that he became the world's worst loser. When he lost, he cried like a howling monkey, beat his chest and kicked the floor. He punched the walls and slapped his opponents, tore off his clothes, chewed the carpet, kicked small pets, screamed till his cheeks went purple and wrenched out his hair in great big chunks!

At school he had no friends, because they were all scared of him. When he lost his temper there was no saying what he might do. In football, when he missed a tackle and the other team scored a goal, he blamed everyone else for getting in his way, then ran amok with the white line marker, until the pitch looked like it was tied up with string. In the playground, when his conker was exploded by another boy's conker, he claimed he wasn't ready and insisted on having one free swipe with his Thunderblaster, which wasn't a conker at all, but a sledgehammer. In the locker room, when he lost at noughts and crosses, he screwed up the paper and forced the winner to swallow it so that the game "never happened". And when the boy chundered, Bruce made him swallow it back down again! And on the tennis court, when he lost a point, he broke his racquet, called the linesman a "Fat blind bat!" and cut the net in half with a hedge trimmer.

"Now listen, Bruce," said the Tasmanian games teacher who was umpiring the match. "Winning is not what's important." Bruce stared at him like he was talking Martian-speak. "We can't all be good at sports. Some of us are better at *other* things – writing stories, acting the giddy goat, naming flowers, singing arias, painting with pasta . . . you get my point? Accept who you are, Bruce. Be the best at what you *can* do." He turned back to his microphone and addressed the small crowd of parents. "Stanley leads 5—"

"Don't say it!" Bruce interrupted, bursting into tears like a baby sucking onions.

"Say what?"

"The score."

"I'm the umpire. It's my job. Stanley leads 5—"

"You're embarrassing me!" blubbed Bruce. "I'll bite you if you say it."

"It's only a game!" said the teacher firmly. "Stanley leads 5-love."

Bruce sank his teeth into the umpire's leg and was sent home before the blood was dry.

Shane and Sheila would not admit defeat. They were winners after all! They had set out to make their son a winner, and a winner he would be! They taught him a hard lesson. If Bruce couldn't win by fair means it was his duty to cheat.

At Sports Day the next week, Bruce ran the three-legged race with a broom instead of a partner.

"But that's cheating," said one of the other children, indignantly.

"It's not cheating," sneered Bruce, "it's so I can run faster and win. If you'd just use that tiny brain of yours for one second you'd work out that another person tied to my leg would just slow me down!" Meanwhile, on the other side of the track, Sheila and Shane were having their ears bent by the Tasmanian tennis teacher.

"Something's got to change," he said, as the gun fired for the start of the race. "He's the worst loser I've ever seen. He has to learn that he can't always be the best!"

"Why?" asked Shane. "He *is* the best, because he *comes* from the best. We're the best parents in the world!"

"Come on, Brucie!" Sheila's foghorn of a voice could empty a compost heap of worms. "If he won't let you pass, trip him up with your broomstick!"

"The point of playing games is to have fun," protested the teacher. "If you win, that's great, but it shouldn't matter if you lose!"

"Kick him! Kick him! Ram the pole in his ear! No, don't try. . . Oh!" Sheila groaned as

Bruce finished last and limped over to join them. He was never short of an excuse or two when he lost. There was always something in his eye or something in his shoe or something itchy up his billabong.

"Yeah, got a pulled muscle thingy there," he muttered limply. "The grass was too green, the broom handle gave me a splinter, and I needed a pee all the way round!" Hot, stinging tears ran down his cheeks. "They ganged up on me and wouldn't let me pass."

"That's called racing," said the teacher.

"That's cheating!" shouted Bruce. "They knew I was the best, so they didn't let me win."

"Well don't stand there blubbing like a girl," hissed Shane. "You're a man, Bruce. If *I* was robbed of victory, *I'd* do something about it."

"Like what?" spluttered the matchstick boy.

"Like find the hammer-thrower's hammer and drop it on the winner's foot!"

"Yeah," grinned his mother. "Smash his little bones into dust. That'll teach the dirty cheat not to beat you again!"

*

By the time the boy's foot came out of plaster, Bruce had been banned from playing games at school.

"He's a bad loser," pronounced the headmaster, "and there's no room for bad losers at this school!"

A week later the school burnt down and Bruce was asked to leave. And because of his record of bad behaviour, other schools refused to take him in, which meant that within two weeks Bruce had lost everything, except his parents, his little sister Kitty, and their house on stilts.

Poor Kitty! The fact that Bruce spent all his time at home from then on, meant that she was now the sole recipient of his nasty attentions. The trouble was that she didn't care a flying auk about winning or losing. She liked flowers and fluffy cloud-paintings in the sky. This suited boastful Bruce right down to the ground. There could be nobody easier to beat than his weedy little sister, who couldn't even throw a tennis ball beyond the end of her shoes!

He challenged Kitty to all sorts of games that he knew she couldn't win, on account of him being twice her age, twice her weight and twice her height. He mashed her at kick-boxing, basketball, koala-lifting, saying the alphabet backwards, spider-chasing, and dragging-a-5kg-bag-of-potatoes-up-the-outdoor-ladder-in-the-fastest-time. Kitty didn't understand the rules of the last one.

"No, Bruce. Not *how* do I do it. *Why!* What's the point?"

"Because I'm the strongest, that's why!" he hollered.

"But we know that already!" she sighed. "So we don't need to drag potatoes up ladders to prove it!"

"Then I am the winner!" Bruce crowed, punching the air and pushing his leering face into Kitty's. "The great and glorious winner! And you are the sad little loser! I'm the best and you're the worst! I'm good and you're bad! I'm handsome and you're ugly!"

"You're pathetic," Kitty said as she skipped up the ladder into the house.

"No. That's *you!*" Bruce shouted after her, but it didn't sound convincing.

Sometimes he made up games so that only he knew the rules. Then if she started to win he could change them. They played Emu Croquet, in which the hoop was made by the emu's curved neck when its head was buried in the sand. But Kitty's ball hit the emu on the ear and when it knocked her to the ground and bit her, Bruce declared himself the winner by one fall and a submission.

They travelled into the outback to play Bush-Snooker, where the object of the game was to whack a rolled-up hedgehog into a kangaroo's pouch. The kangaroo was tied down for Bruce's go and he scored five hedgies in a row, followed by a double roller, a roo-poo and a bat in the basket. But when it was Kitty's go to hit the hedgehog, Bruce said it was, "that time in the game to Bounce the Pouch," and he untied the kangaroo, which promptly hopped off leaving Kitty nothing to aim at. Apparently, this made Bruce the winner.

When they played Trivial Barbecues, Bruce asked Kitty all sorts of questions about barbecues to which nobody could possibly have known the answers. Questions like, "Who invented fire?" And when Kitty answered, "Prehistoric Man," he said, "Yeah, but what was his name?" She didn't know. Neither did Bruce, but he didn't have to answer it. He got the easy questions like, "Bruce, do you cook meat on a barbecue?" "Yes. Two points. I win!"

And sometimes they played ordinary games and Bruce made sure he won by cheating. When they played dominoes, he took Kitty's hamster hostage, and threatened to bury it alive with a nail through its head if she didn't let him lay the last piece. When they played table football, he disabled her goalie with chewing gum. When they got ready for bed after their bath, he called it a race and put a big black spider into Kitty's pyjamas so that he'd be ready first.

Then one day Kitty had had enough. They must have played a million games and Bruce had won them all. He was cock-a-hoop and was forever running round the room punching the air and whooping. Kitty tried not to let it get to her, but it was hard. Her brother's transformation from sad sap to world champion of everything had made him unpleasantly cocky. Bruce had become a bold-hearted braggart who thought he was halfway to God! He strutted around the stilted house with a smug, self-satisfied smile on his face, like he was King of the World.

"I'm the best!" he said to Kitty. "I'm the greatest human being what ever played games. You're just a bug by comparison. A titchy witchetty! You're nothing!"

Kitty could have forgiven him anything, but boasting was nasty. She wanted to take him on. She wanted to prove him wrong. She *was* somebody. She was Kitty! For the first time in her life she wanted to win. She'd have liked to have popped him one on his big fat gob, but she knew he'd only hit her harder, so instead she said, "Why don't we ever play board games?"

Bruce stopped celebrating and jumped off the sofa. "We can play board games," he said warily, but he didn't mean it.

Over the months, Kitty had sussed that there

was one type of game Bruce had never played. Board games. "I bet I can beat you," she smirked mischievously.

"Of course you can't," Bruce swaggered. "You can't beat an egg!"

"So why are you trembling?" she asked.

"I'm not!" he barked, but he was. Kitty had produced a game of Snakes and Ladders.

"Is it because you're scared you might lose?" she giggled. "Is it because you play it with dice?"

Bruce had broken out into a sweat. It *was* the dice. He never played anything with dice, because dice relied on chance, and where there was chance there was always the possibility that he might lose, and Bruce was not a loser. Not any more. He had a reputation to maintain.

"I'm waiting," she said. On the other hand, he hadn't lost a game for two months, so why should he lose one now? It was only his squitty little sister! He took the board off Kitty and opened it on to the table. Besides, if he got into a pickle, he'd just cheat!

"You can start," he said magnanimously, rolling the dice across the board.

Kitty threw a six, then a five and whipped up the first ladder. He threw a three and stayed where he was. She threw another six, missed two snakes, climbed a second ladder, threw a two and was already halfway home, while he threw a one and barely moved. He glowered at his lucky sister and left the dice on his side of the board so that she'd have to reach across for it.

"Can't you pass it?" she asked.

"No," he said. "Get it yourself." The bad-tempered loser was waking up again. She rolled a four and hit the next ladder.

"That's not fair!" he screamed. "I'm changing the rules."

"You can't do that," said Kitty.

"Who's going to stop me?" he snarled. "From now on you go down ladders and up snakes." Kitty had three ladders between her and the finish, whereas Bruce had fifteen snakes he could climb up. He threw a six, hopped up one snake, threw another six, hopped up a second, and finished with a four, putting him just behind Kitty.

"Your go," he grinned.

"Fine," she said, throwing a five and leaping over two ladders in one go. "I'm nearly there." And then it happened. Bruce threw a two and hit the top of a ladder.

"Down you go," laughed his sister. "Down ladders, up snakes!" His face clouded over. His mouth set square. His hands trembled.

"But those *aren't* the rules!" he hissed. "Don't you know nothing? You can only go down snakes!" Kitty couldn't believe it.

"But you said. . ."

"Nothing! I said nothing! Rules are rules! You're the one who's breaking them!" Bruce's eyebrows were twitching, his eyes were red and puffy, he was tugging at his hair like a haunted man. He'd spent so long winning he'd forgotten what it felt like to lose! "I can do anything I want," he screamed, as the bad loser inside his head took control. He picked up the board and crossed to the front door. "I can go up and down ladders and snakes any way I like!" And with that he hurled the board off the balcony and tripped over the pet koala. He grabbed for the handrail, but missed. And the next thing he knew, he had slipped into space and was sliding down the ladder towards the ground, where a hissing frenzy of snakes was waiting to eat him.

Fast Food

The ambulance screamed through the dawn hedgerows. Its blue light winked against the clouds. Its tyres splashed mud across a five-bar gate shut tight with pink string. Inside the screaming bubble, wires hung from the roof like the tentacles of a jellyfish, a black box beeped, a drip swung on a hook and slapped the paramedic's head.

"We're losing him!" came the urgent cry, as she snatched the needle from her colleague and called for more space.

"I need to speak to him first," insisted the policeman.

"No chance."

A hand stayed the wrist that held the needle. "What he has to say may save other lives!" The words hung between them like ice crystals on an Eskimo's clothes line.

"Ten seconds. No more!"

The policeman turned to the patient, his pencil poised. "Why?" he asked. "I just need to know why?"

"I was hungry," whispered the flattened patient.

"But you're too small to eat cars."

"It didn't look big when I first saw it."

"Of course it didn't look big! It was over a mile away down the road."

The patient started to choke and the paramedic moved the policeman to one side.

"It's not fair," gasped the patient. "Everyone else in the world eats fast food."

"Yes, but not when it's doing seventy!" she said, as the arm suddenly went limp and the patient slipped away.

The siren was switched off. The screaming stopped. The hedgehog was dead.

Sock Shock

Socks keep toes and feet warm in the winter, and cool (if freshly laundered) in the summer. Socks stop blisters, pad sporting heels and sometimes match the garish jumpers and handkerchiefs of the rich and famous. Socks can be used to store fifty-pence pieces, to cover golf clubs or to strain out the bits in crab-apple jelly. In most houses, socks are as big a part of Christmas as tangerines, white beards, chocolate logs and figgy pudding. Sometimes they smell, but they never get up and walk on their own (despite what your mothers may tell you), and some exceptionally lucky socks receive permanent makeovers into glove puppets. But generally, in a civilized society that still designs clothes for specific parts of the body, socks are made for one reason and one reason only – for wearing *under* shoes. That is the point of socks!

Nick was a boy who thought differently. Nick was an obstinate boy who liked to do things his own way. There was no reasoning with him. If there was an urgent hurry to leave the house, Nick would choose that "leaving moment" to take a shower. If there was only brown bread for toast, Nick would crave white and would have to visit the shops *immediately* to buy some. If it was 43°C in the shade he'd wear long trousers. If it was freezing, shorts. If a sign said: *DANGER. NO ENTRY. TREE FELLING OVERHEAD. PEDESTRIANS PLEASE FIND ALTERNATIVE ROUTE.* Nick would walk directly underneath the chainsaw with his own sign on his head: *DANGER. NO BRANCH DROPPING. BOY WALKING UNDERNEATH. TREE FELLERS PLEASE FIND ALTERNATIVE TREES.* He wore hats upside down and back to front, he kept stick insects in his lampshade, he painted his bedroom black and temporarily lost the door, and when a man came to the front door selling dusters and ironing board covers, Nick offered him a bed for the night and cooked him supper.

The thing was, Nick did not like wearing shoes on his feet. They were always too tight, too slippery or too pinched. But he didn't like bare feet either. Bare feet were too cold on marble floors, too painful on gravel paths, too splintery on bare floorboards, too muddy in fields of cows, too dog-dooey on pavements, and too exposed to broken toes in a cricket net. This left Nick in something of a dilemma. He hated shoes and he hated bare feet. So Nick wore socks instead. All the time!

Now put yourself in his mother's shoes (something Nick had *never* done). Every day, she spent six hours darning holes, stitching seams, patching elastic and scrubbing dirt, and every week, the holeyest socks had to be replaced at huge cost (a cost so huge that the family had *never* had a holiday). Nick never took his socks off. He wore socks without shoes for school, for soccer, for skateboarding, for shopping, for swimming parties and for soft-sock shuffling. He wore them in all types of weather. In summer, the soles were stained bright green from freshly mown grass. In spring, they were caked in bunny rabbit droppings. In winter, they sucked up rain like blotting paper and flapped and slapped around his ankles like Wee Willie Winkie's night-cap.

So, we have established that Nick liked socks. Then, one day, while Nick's socks were washing in the washing-machine and Nick was keeping guard in case a sock thief should sneak through the cat flap, the machine coughed. It stuttered briefly. For a fraction of a second, the whining cut out in mid-cycle and the drum stopped spinning. Imagine this. You have red hair. You are standing in the middle of the garden. You can hear the constant buzzing of a bee as it flies from one side of the garden to the other. Halfway across it sees your hair. It thinks you are a large red rose. It lands on your hair and stops buzzing, but half a second later it realizes its mistake and flies off, buzzing again. That's what Nick's washing-machine sounded like. Noise – a flicker of silence – noise. He thought no more about it until he opened the time-release door, took out his socks and discovered to his horror that one was missing. One half of a precious pair!

Nick immediately called the police and filed a Missing Sock Report. He filled out a detailed description of the sock and handed over its twin to have its photograph taken for a poster.

HAVE YOU SEEN THIS SOCK?
Hose the thief?
Call Sockland Yard now in strictest confidence!

With a Sock Counsellor standing by in case Nick should suddenly suffer *Delayed Sock Trauma*, the sockless boy climbed inside the machine with a fingerprint kit and dusted the steel drum for evidence of a break-in. But when he climbed back out his face was grim.

The sock thief was clever. His fingerprints had been washed off.

Who had done this to Nick? Was it the Sock Mafia, run by Don Cottononly, who had stolen a sock to stuff up the mouth of a squealing supergrass? Was it the legendary One Sock Goblin, the fearsome fiend of the Underwear, the most evil creature that ever crawled out of the slime – the beast that stole single socks from washing-machines the world over, and used their rank stench to track down their owners and murder them horribly in their beds? Or was it a sinister plot, masterminded by his mum, to stop him wearing socks without shoes?

But before Nick could decide, forty long fingers flashed out of the washing-machine, grabbed his hair and yanked him back inside. Nick was dragged head-first through the five-centimetre waste disposal pipe. His body was squashed into the shape of a plum tomato and shot through the pipe like a hoovered-up rat, before being spat out into a dark, claustrophobic cave that smelt like a goat pit.

He hit the ground with a hard thump. Two red eyes blinked in the darkness and Nick got a whiff of sour breath and unwashed socks.

"So," croaked a gruff voice only centimetres from Nick's ear, "we meet at last."

Nick screamed, jumped to his feet, and stubbed his toe on a stone wall. "That'll teach you to wear shoes!" roared the voice.

"Who are you?" Nick yowled as he hopped up and down on the spot. "What do you want?"

A match was struck. A hurricane lamp was lit. Nick gasped as the flickering light revealed the most hideously terrifying sight that he had ever seen! Standing a metre away from him, in a cave no bigger than a stationery cupboard, was a man-eating goblin with gnarled, warty skin like a toad's! The long-armed, forty-fingered beast was half a metre tall, with a huge lolling head, bulbous eyes and sharp, pointed teeth that click-clacked like claws tapping gravestones. It was holding the stolen sock in its gnarled fist and was sniffing its pungent aroma through two black holes in the middle of its face. It looked like its nose had been chopped off. But when a green tongue suddenly flicked out of the left-hand hole, Nick started to cry.

"Are you the . . . erm. . ." He could barely bring himself to utter those terrifying words, ". . .the One Sock Goblin?"

"I am!" roared the beast, lunging forward to give Nick an up-close view of his tonsils.

"Are you a crunching, munching, lunching goblin too?" the boy wailed.

"I am the only sock-stealing goblin ever made! Look around you," it cackled. "See the tunnels?" Nick's body was paralysed with fear, but he could still move his eyeballs. Behind the sock racks, the walls were peppered with tiny holes. "Each tunnel leads to the back of every washing machine in the world," snorted the brute. "This allows me to sneak in the out-pipe and steal one sock from everyone."

"And then you murder the owners in their beds!" wailed Nick. "You sniff them out and plunge their heads into boiling oil! You tear out their hearts and feed their lungs to the crows! You split them in half and chop off their limbs with a swordfish!"

"How did you know?" mocked the goblin. "That's exactly what I do." Tears were streaming down Nick's face.

"Is it because I never wear shoes?" he squeaked. "Am I to be punished because I wear socks all the time and make extra work for my mummy?"

"Could be!" winked the goblin.

"So when are you going to kill me?" Nick screamed, and the goblin screamed back,

"Never!"

"Where did you get these fanciful ideas from?" the goblin asked Nick a few minutes later when the boy had calmed down. "Boiling oil, crows, swordfish! I mean how could I possibly kill you? I'm only a quarter your size!" Nick was confused. "I collect socks," said the beast. "Doesn't that tell you something about me? When was the last time someone was murdered for their socks?"

"Never?" ventured Nick.

"Precisely," said the sock goblin.

"So why do you steal them then?"

"I run a worm hospital," it explained, "for unfortunate worms that are injured by gardening forks or birds' beaks. I find socks make ideal sleeping bags."

"And that's where all the single socks go when they disappear from washing machines? To make sleeping bags for worms?"

"Well, worms have got to sleep somewhere," explained the goblin. "And I never take two socks, because worms are fiercely individualistic creatures and insist on having different-coloured beds. Now, if you'll excuse me, I've got a television crew arriving to make a documentary about the worm hospital. I'm being interviewed by Rolf Harris, actually."

"But what about me?" asked Nick. "How do I get back?"

"The way you came in," said the goblin, taking out a mirror and painting its eyelashes with mascara. It caught Nick staring. "One has to make the best of what one's got," it grinned. "For the camera. Goodbye." But Nick wouldn't leave, not before he'd asked the goblin one more question.

"Why did you bring me here?" he said.

"An honest mistake. I heard you in the drum and thought you were a sock."

Nick was still confused. "So you're not working for my mother? You're not going to call on the powers of darkness and use spooky spells and witchcraft to force me to wear shoes?"

It was the goblin's turn to look puzzled. "No," it said.

So Nick never did.

He still wears socks without shoes, which only goes to prove that wearing socks without shoes can't be the worst sin on earth, or somewhere out there the worst fiend on earth would have been created to put a stop to it. And another thing – if we listen to gossip, we can scare ourselves silly over nothing. At least that's what I've heard.

But just in case I've got my facts wrong, promise me one thing. Don't go hunting for lost socks in the washing machine. You can never *truly* know what else might be in there.

Revenge of the Bogeyman

On a scale of one to ten for bodily disgustingness this tale is fifteen and climbing. It is, I'm afraid, about PLF – picking, licking and flicking. It is dedicated to all children (whatever their age) who have devoted their lives to the private art of Beak Burrowing. That is to say, those of you with fingers like trowels who poke and prod, worm and wiggle, dig and delve, scoop and scrape, and riddle and rake until you get a nosebleed!

Is everyone now clear as to where this story is going?

It is universally acknowledged that picking one's nose in broad daylight is not the best way to get served in a restaurant. But Dee Doodah, known as Digger Dee Doodah to her friends, would pick her nose anywhere.

In an Oyster Bar, she picked and flicked a grisly green-gilbert over her shoulder and on to a plate on the waiter's tray. She *tried* to tell the customer that it wasn't an oyster he was eating, that it was one of her bogeys in a shell, but he refused to believe her and slurped it down with a glass of champagne. She picked her nose on stage, during concerts for the school orchestra. Never one to waste time, she liked to excavate her nostrils at the same time as playing her violin. But one night, during a particularly frenetic passage in *The Flight of the Bumble Bee* she stuck the bow up her nose by mistake. You should have heard her scream. But more to the point, you should have seen the size the bogey she pulled out on the end of the bow. It catapulted across the orchestra pit, stuck to the conductor's baton, and in his frantic efforts to flick it off, he waved his baton all over the place, lost time, rhythm and pace, and *The Flight of the Bumble Bee* crashed and burned.

And once, she even picked her nose in front of a beautiful princess and held her hand out for a shake. Fortunately the princess spotted the nostril-log just in time and Dee was wrestled to the ground by a bogeyguard.

The only time that Digger Dee would *not* pick her nose was when horses were present. She thought it was mean to tease them, because horses cannot fit their hooves up their hooters.

Her parents were naturally appalled. Little girls were supposed to smell sweetly of soap and honey. Little girls were supposed to be pretty. Little girls were supposed to be well behaved. But *their* daughter rammed her fists up her noseholes like an uncouth boy! Uncouth boys thought it was funny to spit their pickings at passing cyclists, but little girls were supposed to be more refined. Not Dee though. She holed and rolled with the best of them. She kept lists in her bedroom of her biggest bogeys, and one wall was covered in red crosses. This was her Olympic Wall, where she measured how high she could flick them. It was a bit like the shot-put only different. She called it the snot-put.

Whenever her parents complained about Dee flicking green ones around the house, she said, "Would you prefer me to eat them?"

"No!" grimaced her mother, who felt sick at the thought. "It's just that loose bogeys have a tendency to stick to household objects. I found one in the middle of a cake that I baked the other day."

"Yum," said Dee.

"And one on your father's bald patch!"

"He could have used it to stick a wig on," Dee said.

That night her father stuck on his sternest face and made an angry, chin-wobbling speech at dinner.

"Stop winkling!" he shouted. Dee had her finger so far up her nose she looked as if she was trying to pick her own brain. "Now listen to me, Dee. If you carry on digging at the rate you're digging now, you will eventually dig so deep that you will dig out. . ." he paused to add weight to the next two words, ". . .the bogeyman!" Dee gasped. Her mother shrieked. The finger fell from the nosehole.

"The bogeyman! What does he do?" shivered Dee.

"*That* you do not want to know!" growled her father. He was right. What the bogeyman did was best left a secret.

Breaking a bad habit, however, is often easier said than done. Although Dee tried to stop picking her nose she couldn't. At night, while she slept, her ferreting finger developed a will of its own. It poked and prodded the inside of her nostrils like a dog digging for bones.

Then one night, she woke with a start. The room was empty. The window was closed, but there was a soft, faraway voice filling her head with cotton-wool words.

"Dig deeper," it hissed. "There's gold in that there nose, Dee! There's buried treasure! Dig deeper, Dee. Pick faster. There's magic in them bogeys!"

Dee climbed out of bed and checked behind

the curtains, but there was nobody there. Then she went to the mirror above the sink, tipped back her head and checked up her nose for treasure. Empty. Not even a gold sovereign or a precious book about ponies. But as she returned to bed the voice started up again. "Dig!" it sighed. "Dig now! Dig like you've never dug before!" The temptation was too great. Dee's fingers were already twitching and at the first sign of mental weakness, they plunged up her nostrils and started to pick.

After half an hour of deep-conk-delving and root-cartilage-scraping, Dee felt a big sticky one lodged inside a sinus. She managed to pinch it between thumb and forefinger and to jiggle it free of the bone. It *was* a big one. It came out with a satisfying plop. Dee rolled it up and flicked it at the wall, where it slid down towards her bed like a thick, slimy slug.

Then suddenly it stopped. Dee was transfixed. It started to steam like a sizzling Chinese dumpling. Then it rolled sideways. It zipped from one corner of the room to the other, leaving smoking black tracks across the paper. And then it stopped again. Dee thought it must be dead (if a bogey could be alive to begin with). She expected it to fall, but instead of coming unstuck, it flipped inside out. It twisted and turned until it looked like a green Yorkshire pudding – only, name me one Yorkshire pudding with arms!

Digger Dee's jaw crashed down on to her trembling knees. She was gobsmacked. Her bogey not only had long green arms, but two green legs as well, and a face – a face like green nutty chocolate, and rough, spotty skin like a gecko's.

"I am fed up with your fingers!" said the creature as it stepped off Dee's bed, leaving a nasty green puddle behind it. Up close, Dee could see short stubby hairs all over its body.

"Are you the fearful bogeyman?" she quivered.

"Indeed I am, young lady, and you are in a whole heap of trouble!" The monstrous slimeball laid a pickaxe down on the bed and Dee whimpered.

"But a little voice told me to pick you," she squeaked.

"That was me," slurped the snotty monster. "For ten years I have put up with your fingers trying to evict me from my home. I'd had enough. I needed you to dig me out so that I could have a word."

"I'm listening," she said meekly.

"And mind you do," he growled, pushing her into a chair with his finger and leaving a gob of goo on her pyjamas. "How would you like it if I came along with a bulldozer and turfed you out of *your* house every five minutes?"

"Not much," whispered Dee.

"If every time you climbed into the bath, a huge finger poked through the window and tried to scrape you up the tiles? If every time you sat down to breakfast, your back door was pushed in. If you had to sleep surrounded by a steel cage for fear of being plucked from your bed? If you had carry a heavy pickaxe all the time, just in case you *were* snatched and needed something to grip onto the walls with?" (So that's what the pickaxe was for – nostril gripping.)

"I don't think I'd like it at all," Dee whimpered.

"No!" roared the bogeyman. "And neither do I!"

"Are you upset?" she asked nervously.

"Too right, I'm upset!" he shouted, spraying the room with tiny green globules. "Just because we're small and easily flicked doesn't mean that bogeys don't have feelings too, you know. Now, are you going to stop picking on me or am I going to have to make you?" The question came out of the blue and took Digger Dee by surprise. She wasn't thinking straight.

"But I love picking my nose," she blurted, which was precisely the wrong answer. There was a gurgle in the back of the bogeyman's throat. Then his sticky fingers clenched into sticky fists and a glistening film of green slime oozed through his skin like sweat.

"Right," he said. And he grabbed Dee by the arm and ate her.

It all happened so quickly that Dee didn't even have time to scream. One moment she was sitting in her bedroom, the next she was hurtling down a gummy green throat and popping out into a huge cave. The white walls were smooth and full of polished holes. It wasn't stone. It felt more like bone, but before Dee could work out exactly where she was, a loud scratching noise, like rough sandpaper being scraped across human skin, thundered in her ears. The ground shook, the cave tilted and the floor became a slide. She fell and slipped backwards, but there was nothing to cling on to. If only she had the bogeyman's pickaxe!

"Help!" Her feet slithered downhill. She skidded round a sharp bend into a steep pink tunnel. It was like surfing down a flume in a waterpark. Another bend, another straight, she flipped up and over like a crashing bobsleigh, and then as she raced round the final turn she saw a huge red boulder directly in front of her. At least it looked like a boulder – only boulders didn't move and this one was twitching. It was scratching. It was scraping. It was poking and prodding. Dee realized with horror that it wasn't a boulder at all. It was the tip of a very large pink finger and *she* was its target! Too late! It scooped her out of the cave like a winkle flipped from its shell.

Digger Dee Doodah found herself perched on the finger of a giant. She was covered in cobwebs of tacky gloop and had just been picked from his nose. The giant examined her closely, then rolled her between his finger and thumb and flicked her at the wall. He thought she was a bogey! Dee screamed as she spun through the air and the wall tumbled up to splat her.

"Oomph!" The impact knocked the wind out of her lungs. She slid down the wall on to the floor where she was promptly trodden on by the giant's wife. "Help!" wailed Dee. "I'm under your shoe!" But her voice was so tiny that the giantess didn't hear her. The great lolloping lump just stomped across the room flattening Dee flatter than a blob of chewing gum. "I'm not a bogey!" she sobbed, as the giantess stopped by the cooker and stamped on the bellows that kept the fire roaring.

The sharp kicking movement knocked Dee

off the shoe and she fell into a bowl of water. Only to Dee it was more like a lake, and the lake's owner was a huge, hairy, *thirsty* dog. The bearded mutt bent down to take a drink and saw teeny tiny Dee swimming. It only meant to prod her with its paw, but she was so tiny that its prod was like a head-on blow from a battering ram. Dee shot out of the water like a pebble skimming off the sea, skidded along the kitchen table and banged her head on the marmalade jar. She came to rest, wet, bruised and disorientated, with her legs in the air and her face squashed against a china bowl. A bottle of milk banged down on to the table next to her and narrowly missed crushing her legs. Above the bottle was the face of the giant's ugly son, who was scoffing cereal.

Dee had to get out of there. Boys were fiercely brutal flickers and if he thought she was a bogey, there was no saying how far he might flick her. The shadow of a huge hand drained the light from her face as the boy crammed his fat gob. Drips of milk fell from his mouth like heavy rain. Dee started to run, but the movement caught the boy's eye and he swatted at her with his hand. Dee had seen the fist coming. She dived towards the lip of the table, somersaulted over the edge and hid on a ledge underneath. Above her head, stuck to the underside of the wooden table were rows of solid black logs. This was the son's secret stash, where he stored his unwanted pickings!

Suddenly, the boy's massive fingers plunged under the table. She swayed out of the way as they scraped past her shoulder, but they must have felt her arm, because they slid back towards her. Dee had to move. She crouched down to make herself even smaller and ran along a wooden ledge towards the table leg, but a thumb blocked her path and flicked her into the palm of a hand.

"Well, well, well," laughed the giant's son, lifting Dee into the light. "Don't remember putting this bogey under the table. Nice fat one and all."

"I am NOT fat!" screamed Dee, but the boy couldn't hear her.

"Don't mind if I do," he said. And without a thought for hygiene or manners, or Dee for that matter, he popped the girl-gilbert into his mouth. She hurled herself out of the way as his huge yellow teeth chomped up and down like a monstrous pulping machine. Saliva squirted from the wet walls as she flattened herself against the pink floor that rolled up and down like the deck of a storm-tossed boat. She couldn't hang on. She was being sucked towards a huge black hole at the back. His throat! Dee was going to be swallowed! She had to do something quickly! With the sound of the giant's heartbeat thumping in her ears she knelt down, wiped her mouth and bit the giant tongue as hard as she could. The big boy yelled and spat Dee out. She shot across the room like a bullet and fell into the arms of the bogeyman, who was looking rather smug.

"Now do you get it?" he asked.

"I do," she said.

"Now do you see how dangerous the world can be for bogeys when we're PLF'ed?"

"I do," she said.

"And do you swear never ever to pick your nose and put a poor bogey's life at risk again?"

Digger Dee looked the bogeyman full in his squitty eyes. "I do," she said.

And with that he grabbed her hand and whisked her back through time and space until he reached her bedroom.

"Thank you," she said, as the bogeyman crawled back up her nose.

"My pleasure," he replied, pushing a thick bush of hair out of his way. "Just remember to be properly respectful of all bogey rights in future." Dee nodded. "Because all of us need somewhere to live." The bogeyman's voice echoed like a cry in a canyon as he climbed up the inside of her nostril and made his way home to Mount Sinus.

"Ow!" yelped Dee.

"Sorry!" said the squeak in her head. "I slipped. Had to use the pickaxe."

Digger Dee Doodah never picked her nose again. To begin with the urge was hard to resist, but more recently, since she started picking her ears, it has not been that bad.

Trouble is, there's only a centimetre to go before she digs up the waxwoman. *Then* she'll be sorry!

Crocodile Tears

The Howling household was damper than your average home. Herbie Howling was a man who loved his family. In fact he loved his family so much that every time his wife or daughter did something – even if it was only reading a newspaper or making a cup of tea or walking through a door – he was overcome with such gut-wrenching pride that he gushed tears like a big, sobbing baby. Cissie Howling, his wife, shed tears of quite a different sort. She was a nervous wreck and jumped neurotically from one imaginary crisis to another. She wept tears of terror morning, noon and night. Spiders didn't help, but gas bills, front door bells, carpet stains, fast-moving pets, can openers, sheets that wouldn't crease straight, and her tearful daughter's hand-kerchief pile all reduced her to tears in seconds. Gwendolyn was that tearful daughter. She had learnt everything she knew from her soft, over-sensitive parents. She was a nasty, manipulative child, who used tears as a weapon to get whatever it was she wanted.

"What's the matter with my Weepy Wen?" wept her father. Seeing his daughter cry always made *him* cry too.

"I've got too much homework to do," blubbered Gwendolyn, "I think it might be going to give me a headache!"

"Eek!" cried her father. Then, "Nooooo!" His face paled as his huge frame juddered. "Not a headache. Please, Wen, tell me it's not a headache!"

"But Daddy," trembled the wet-eyed Wen. "It *is* a headache!"

"A headache!" This time the wail was Cissie's. "What do we think has caused it?" she whimpered. "Oh, how shall I survive if my only daughter is taken ill? Do we think it's something serious? Do you think there's a possibility you might d-d-d. . ." The D word stuck in her quavering throat. She couldn't say it out loud.

"I want you to know," Gwendolyn sobbed, "that you have been the sweetest, dearest parents a girl could ever have hoped for!"

"It *is* serious!" bawled Cissie. "I can tell."

"It might be –" snivelled Gwendolyn, as her father wept copiously into the velveteen curtains and wrung them out on the patio – "*unless* you let me bunk off my homework –" she hesitated to wipe a big rolling tear from her cheek – "for that is the only way I can avoid the head pain!"

Then, as Gwendolyn broke down again, her howling parents fell upon her shoulder and beseeched her, in the name of all that was sacred to their family, to promise them that she would *not*, under any circumstances, touch her wretched homework that night. Gwendolyn's bottom lip wobbled like a springboard, and even though her eyes were misty with tears, she forced a brave smile, sniffed courageously and nodded her assent. For the sake of her parents' peace of mind, she would selflessly abandon her homework!

You *do* see how it worked, don't you?

"Daddy, can I have a new dress?" No tears = No dress.

"Daddy, *(facial muscles twitch)* can *(nostrils flare)* I *(lips chewed)* have *(sobs build)* a new *(collapse into wailing)* dress?"

"If it means that much to you, Gwenny Wenny, of course you can, my pretty little angel."

Tears made all the difference, and Gwendolyn had every tear known to man, woman and child in her armoury. . .

She could do temper tantrum.

"I won't get in the back of the car. I won't! It makes me feel sick. I want to ride in the front next to Daddy, so that people think I'm a woman!"

"But your mother prefers it in the front."

"Waaaaaaaah! Boooooo hooooo! My cheeks are going to burst if you don't let me!"

"I'll go in the back," howled her mother in distress, while Herbie banged his tortured head on the bonnet and wept buckets down the metallic paintwork for being such a wicked father and nearly saying "No" to his daughter.

She could do "poor, pathetic me!"

"Oh, nobody loves me," she sobbed outside the shoe shop. "I'm so miserable. It's only a teeny tiny pair of shoes. If I had my own money I wouldn't ask you to pay for them, but I am only a little baby child, Daddy, and you *are* my father. . ."

Herbie Howling *always* cried when Gwendolyn called him father. It made him feel protective, like a big, strong, burglar-bashing man.

" . . .so it *is* your job. And when I'm bigger I shall buy you a wheelchair and carpet slippers, but don't let that influence your decision now."

She got the shoes after a mega hugging, kissing and weeping session on the pavement.

She could do pain.

"Oooh! Owww! Agh! Yowser! Yowser!" Then a gasp, a frozen gesture, a melodramatic hand to the mouth, a faint, "I'll be all right!" Another gasp. "No! Nobody must look! It's too gruesome. I think I might have cut my finger clean off! Oooooh! Ow! Might I trouble you for a plaster? And a needle and thread? I won't be a nuisance. I'll sit quietly in the corner and stitch it back on. I'll be fine." Another pause while excruciating pain squeezed glassy tears from her tightly closed eyes. "Might I have an aspirin to take away the pain? Or a Coca Cola or something. A pizza or an ice cream would definitely work. Or a hot dog!" She got the hot dog with extra chilli sauce, and by the time she'd gobbled it all up, causing joyful tears to spring from the eyes of her parents, who loved to watch her eat, her bad finger had miraculously cured itself. There wasn't even a scratch on it.

And she could do volume.

Oh boy, could she do volume! She could pitch over a fire engine. She could scream down a Formula One racing car. She could out-wail a flood warning. Gwendolyn Howling was a professional cry-baby who used her dubious talents to get what she wanted. They weren't real tears. They were made on the spot, squeezed out of bone-dry tear ducts, each one a work of art in its own right. They were crocodile tears and you don't need me to tell you how ruthless a crocodile can be.

One day, just before Christmas, Gwendolyn and her parents were fighting over the television. Cissie and Herbie Howling wanted to watch the news – there was talk of nuclear war between Britain and Plutovia (so nothing too important) – but Gwendolyn wanted to watch a new boy band, Hunx 'n' Chunx, strut their stuff live on the Funk Party.

"Oh, but Daddy, please!" she wailed, burying her head in an embroidered cushion and sneakily rubbing her eyes against the coarse material. When she looked up they were bright red. "My whole life depends on seeing this band. Don't you understand?" She bowed her head as if trying to control her judders. "If I don't see them I shall be ostracized at school. I shall become a loner, friendless and unloved, drifting towards a life of desolation with no GCSEs, neck tattoos and a pit-bull terrier who eats old ladies' sausages!" She burst into a howl at the thought of such a squalid existence. Tears popped out of her eyes and squirted down her face, where they were allowed to drip off the end of her chin and splash to the floor for maximum effect. Her father hovered over the remote control. He glanced at his wife, whose worried lips were twitching. How could they be so cruel to their own flesh and blood!

"Oh, turn it over!" he blurted. The words exploded out of his mouth like water bursting through a dam wall. "I'm such a fiend!"

"Forget the news!" howled her mother. "It's only a nuclear world war. There'll be another. I'm so selfish. Forgive me, Gwenny. Watch your lovely boys. I could never be happy again knowing that I had caused such misery in your life!"

Wen redoubled her tears, switching from "poor, pathetic me!" to "I must be the luckiest girl in the world to have you two saints for parents!" She flung her arms around her father's neck, squeezed her mother's hand and the three of them wept waterfalls in a great big triangle of love. But by the time they had finished and switched over to the Funk Party, Hunx 'n' Chunx had finished their song.

"I'm gutted," choked her father.

"Me too!" wailed her mum, while Wen howled out of the room in a state of emotional hysteria. If she sobbed much more her heart would surely break. At least, that was the impression she gave.

She ran upstairs to the bathroom and turned off the tears like a tap. She didn't care a fig about Hunx 'n' Chunx. All she cared about was getting her own way, and she'd done that. But while she was wiping the crocodile tears from her cheeks and peering at her puffy face in the mirror, she saw something move in the corner of her eye. Something with webbed feet and a yellow bill. It looked like a duck, a teeny tiny duck, no bigger than a pea, and as she peered more closely, it dribbled out of her eye, trapped

inside a glistening tear. She wiped the tear on to
a finger and burst the bubble with a nail. The
diminutive duck opened its tiny bill and spoke
in a soft, watery voice.

"I am a tear duck," it hissed, "born of titch-
witchery. I bring you a warning from Sakusaki,
the Old Croc."

Gwendolyn was so surprised to hear this tiny
creature talk that her mouth fell open.

"You would do well to be scared. He is the
father of all crocodiles, a monstrous, magical
beast torn from a time when sorcery reigned. A
time when crocodile tears were as precious as
diamonds, because only crocodiles cried them.
But the day that children stole the tears for their
own selfish ends, was the day the tears became
worthless. If you continue to spill them,
Sakusaki will have no choice but to take back
what are rightfully his."

"Take back my tears!" sneered Gwendolyn.
"What on earth do you mean?"

The tear duck opened its bill as if to reply,
but instead of words, a glass tear plopped out
into Gwendolyn's palm. It was the size of a

pin-head and swirled inside with white, buffeting clouds. Then suddenly, the clouds parted and the tear blinked. There was an eye inside. It was the green eye of a crocodile and reflected in the pupil was Gwendolyn's face. Her eyes were stuck wide. Her mouth was open. She was screaming with fear.

"Take great care," prophesied the tear duck, reading the glass tear like a crystal ball. "Sakusaki knows where you are. No more faking, or it. . ."

"It will all end in tears!" scoffed Gwendolyn in a bored, know-it-all voice. She had heard grown-ups spin this lie so often that it had ceased to have any meaning. "I'm not three years old, you know," she sneered. "I don't believe you!" And she didn't. She believed that Sakusaki was a myth, that crocodile tears were a GOOD thing because they got her what she wanted, and that a talking duck the size of a pea was just a weird daydream. But when her parents told her to put her coat on, because they were taking her to see a pantomime, and the pantomime was *Peter Pan*, with Captain Hook and the CROCODILE, Gwendolyn had a rethink. The crocodile thing was probably just a coincidence, but why take the risk? After all, she still had plenty of other ammunition to get what she wanted – kicking, sulking, screaming, stomping – she'd just have to cut out the crocodile tears. For the time being.

So when her parents wanted to take a bus to the theatre, and Gwendolyn wanted to ride in a white limousine, she did not cry. She smashed a vase on the telly and burst a cushion instead. When they arrived at the theatre and she wanted the most expensive seats in the house, she trod on the toe of the Lady Mayor, threw herself at the wall and beat her little fists black and blue until her father coughed up the cash. And still no tears. And there were no tears when she screamed for sweets either.

"Oh, yum-bum, tickle my tum! Chocolate! I want a big box of honeycomb centres, some dusty white truffles and a fudge forest!"

"I don't think so," said her mother sensibly. "You'll ruin your dinner." The bottom lip trembled, the cheeks wobbled, the voice started to waver, but no tears.

"But I lo . . . huh-huh . . . ove chocolate!" Wenny whined, drawing stares of disgust and disbelief from fellow theatre-goers. But she hadn't finished yet. "Help!" she shrieked. "Help! My parents beat me!" Her mother blushed with embarrassment, while her sweaty father rushed over from the kiosk with all the chocolates he could carry. "About time," she said gracelessly. "By the way, I'm really looking forward to a raspberry ripple in the interval. And I want a programme now, and some toys!"

Fifty pounds, and much hair-tugging, stair-chewing and mirror-kicking later, and Gwendolyn had a programme, a pair of binoculars, a fluorescent necklace, a big foam finger to point at the baddies and a coat on her seat to raise her up for a perfect view. And still not a tear shed. Her poor father, however, was completely cleaned out. He only had two pounds left and he was saving that for the raspberry ripple.

So, at the interval, when the person in front

of Gwendolyn in the queue bought the last raspberry ripple in the theatre, Herbie and Cissie knew that a rumpus was brewing. Gwenny pulled the woman's hair and called her a greedy pig. "That was mine!" she yelled, but as she did so she felt a well-oiled welling rise in the back of her throat. She recognized the sign. It was a tear, escaping from the depths of her tortured soul! "Get me a raspberry ripple!" she hollered at her spineless, wet-faced father. "And make it snappy!" Speed was of the essence if tears were to be avoided. "Run, run, run!"

He was sprinting down the aisles trying to buy a raspberry ripple from another member of the audience. Suddenly he stopped and leapt in the air. "Bingo!" he shouted, holding the ice-cream aloft.

Wen smiled, the tear subsided and a ripple of relief spread across the audience. Now at last this horrible girl would cease her spoilt antics and they could return to watching the pantomime.

"Wait!" There was still a problem. Her father

had bought a raspberry cone and Gwendolyn wanted a tub.

"But I can't buy you one now," he whimpered, pulling out his empty pockets. "I've no money left!" With one flex of her epiglottis his diabolic daughter let out a supersonic scream that woke the sleeping cherubs on the ceiling and rattled the safety curtain.

"I want a raspberry tub!" she howled, flopping to the floor and kicking her legs like a two-year-old. Then she tossed in a spoilt "Aaaaaaaggggghhhhh!" at the top of her voice just in case there was anybody in the theatre who wasn't paying attention. Her mother and father squirmed, the audience looked the other way, actors poked their heads around the curtain to see what was going on, but no raspberry tub appeared. This was one battle she was *not* going to win. Unless. . . Gwendolyn stopped screaming and thought for a second. Unless she changed tactics and gained the audience's sympathy. If she acted weak and feeble, some kind-hearted person was bound to give her their tub. But sympathy required tears!

There was nothing else for it. Gwendolyn checked the auditorium for crocodiles (the one on stage didn't count – it was only a bloke in a costume) and went for the big blub-down!

The crocodile tears arrived at a rush. They were unstoppable. They pumped out of her eyes, cascaded down her cheeks and dripped into a lapping lake at her feet. The audience softened. No adult can be cross with a crying child. Raspberry tubs were handed along the aisles until she had more than she could carry. The tears were a triumph and Weepy Wen was as pleased as punch. She had won!

Or had she?

Suddenly, she doubled over and clutched her eyes. It felt like they'd just been stabbed with a pin.

"What's happening?" squealed her mother.

"I don't know," she screamed. "There's something in my eye. Take it out! Take it out!"

"Wenny!" wailed her father, treading on toes as he rushed to pick her up. "Show me what's. . ." But he pulled up short when he saw her eyes. "What's wrong?" he gasped. "Your eyes have turned green!" And as he watched, the largest tear that Gwendolyn had ever shed oozed out of her right eye and plinked into her hands. She froze. She knew what she was going to find. The tear duck had warned her. Trapped inside the shimmering dome was Sakusaki, the Old Croc himself!

But far from being the monstrous, magical beast that the tear duck had described, Sakusaki was no bigger than a jelly bean! Gwendolyn roared with laughter.

"To think that I was scared of *you*!" she crowed. "I could squash you with my thumb!"

But when she tried to she cut her thumb badly. The crocodile's skin was as sharp as coral and the blood from the cut dripped over the tear.

In the twinkle of a reptile's eye, the magic crocodile grew until it was three times Gwendolyn's size. Then, with one snap of its powerful jaws, it woofled her up like a tub of ice-cream. The audience gasped with horror. Some even ran for the exits. But when the crocodile cried pretend-tears and wailed in a high-pitched impersonation of Gwendolyn, "Oh now look what I've done. I've gobbled her up by mistake! I'm such a silly billy! I hope I haven't spoiled the pantomime!" the audience stopped and laughed and thought it was part of the show. And when the crocodile took a bow and vanished in a puff of smoke, they thought it was magic and applauded. Nobody seemed to notice that Gwendolyn hadn't come back.

Except for her parents. They were inconsolable and wept for ten years without stopping.

So you see, it *did* all end in tears, after all.

The Pie Man

Donald was a sucker. He entered the world sucking and when his time came to leave he exited that way too. Sucking put Donald in a pie, and this is how it happened.

Silly little suck-a-thumb
Sucks until his digit's numb,
Ignoring what he knows is true;
The Pie Man has a rendezvous.
Crusty, flaky, pastry pie,
Chop a thumb to hold crust high.
Meaty, sweety, bone and nail,
Cures a sucker without fail.

When Donald was born he was sucking his thumb. When Donald was weighed by the nurse he was sucking his thumb. When Donald was cuddled, when Donald was fed, when Donald was changed, when Donald was asleep, when Donald was screaming . . . he was sucking his thumb.

"Why does he do it?" asked his mother.

"Maybe he likes the taste," speculated his father. "Maybe it tastes of chocolate or rice pudding."

"Or stewed apples and custard," rhapsodized the large, West Indian midwife, who loved stewed apples and custard.

"Maybe his thumb's growing out of his gums by mistake," roared his gross Uncle Bert, who thought he was a comedian, but was in fact a bore.

"One thing's for sure," said the midwife, "If he doesn't stop that sucking soon, the Pie Man will come and chop his thumbs off."

"I beg your pardon?" gasped Donald's mother, who was so shocked that she nearly dropped the baby. "Who's the Pie Man?"

"Pie Man, Patty Man, Filo Fella, they're all the same person. He uses little thumbs to hold up the pastry tops on his pies," she explained. "To let the steam out, to keep the pastry crusty."

"Thumbs!" shrieked Donald's mother. "Whose thumbs?"

"Thumb-suckers' thumbs," replied the midwife. "Little, wrinkled, white, tooth-marked thumbs." There was an unholy pause while Donald's mother considered her next question carefully.

"But if he only uses the thumbs to hold up the pastry on his pies," she whispered, "what does he do with the rest of the child?"

"He cuts that off," smiled the midwife. "Thumbs is all he needs. Cheerio, darling! He's a lovely boy. Fine thumbs like sweet bananas!"

On the way home, Donald sucked his thumb with an orchestral range of loud, sloppy, slurpy noises, while his parents brooded on the midwife's gruesome words. Donald's father became really rather cross.

"If the Pie Man tries to perform a double thumbectomy on my son, I'll. . ." he blathered.

"You'll what?" scoffed his wife.

"I'll beat him up," he yelled. "I'll punch his nose. I'll throw water in his face. I'll slap him with a fish-slice!"

"Hardly likely to scare away a supernatural demon, is it?" she said. "There is only one way to protect Donald from this beast and that's to stop the boy from sucking his thumb."

She was right, of course, and Donald's father was rather relieved that he wouldn't have to go head to head with a crazy, half-baked chef who was two blackbirds short of a pie.

The theory was impeccable; in practice, however, it was less easy to achieve. Donald was only one week old and did not *want* to stop sucking his thumb. He did not want to listen to reason either.

"What's the matter with you Donald?" yelled his over-anxious father. "Do you want your thumbs chopped off?"

What did Donald care? He didn't know what

"chopped off" meant, let alone what "thumbs" were. And when his parents wedged their feet against the wall and tried to prise his thumb from his mouth, Donald screamed and cried, and lashed out with his little feet. It was clear to his parents that Donald was no ordinary sucker. He was a super-sucker with a suck more powerful than the single sucker foot of an upside-down ceiling snail. And a suck *that* strong needs to be satisfied! Which was why Donald's parents rushed out and bought him a dummy.

They made the switch at night, while Donald was asleep. They tickled his nose with a feather and, when he opened his mouth to sneeze, they whipped out his thumb and pressed the dummy between his lips. By the time Donald woke up six hours later, he was already used to the rubber teat. He was still sucking, you see, and that was all that mattered.

But what was a perfect solution to the Pie Man problem swiftly developed into a problem of a different sort. As Donald grew up, the dummy became a feature of his face. It remained stuck in his mouth at all times and made him look like a bull with a ring through its nose. He sucked it in the shops, in the park, at school, in the pool, on the bus, at the cinema, at mealtimes, in the choir and once whilst playing blow football. He lost 323-0.

By the time Donald was ten, the dummy was still plugged in his mouth. It was horribly old, disgustingly sticky and somewhat furry round the edges. A dog would not have sucked it, but Donald did. He was addicted.

"He's a dummyholic," announced the doctor. "Stand up, Donald and repeat after me. 'My name is Donald and I'm a dummyholic.'"

"My name is Donald and I'm a dummy-holic," mumbled the boy through his rubber stopper.

"What should we do?" worried his mother. "We tried to take the dummy away from him once, but his unplugged suck destroyed half the sitting room."

"After he'd sucked the ornaments off the shelves and the knobs off the telly," explained

Donald's father, "he sucked the carpet off the floor, the paper off the wall and the door off its hinges."

"That is a powerful suck," acknowledged the doctor, grimly. "But he's old enough to know better now. He's ten years old and still looks like a baby. The dummy must go!"

Donald's parents tried to follow the doctor's orders, but getting rid of the dummy was easier said than done. One night, while Donald was supping his supper through a straw, his father sprang an ambush. He roller-skated through the kitchen, lassoed the dummy with a rope and chucked it in the dustbin. Donald did not move from his seat. Then with one almighty flex of his cheeks, he sucked the dummy back into his gob, bringing a dustbin lid, a fishy skeleton and a rather startled cat crashing through the window after it. His parents buried the dummy under the patio, but Donald hired a mechanical digger and dug it up again. They hurled the dummy on top of a moving bus, but Donald chased it down the street by swinging from lamppost to lamppost like Tarzan. They even fed it to a live snake, but Donald just put his hand straight down the snake's throat, as you would if you were turning a sock inside out, and pulled the dummy back up.

The older Donald became the more embarrassing it was to walk down the street with him and his dummy. Toddlers in nappies bawled for a suck, fussy mothers with hairy legs and principles shot sharp looks of disapproval, old people shook their heads and muttered, "In my day we were lucky to suck on a piece of coal," and a policeman tried to arrest him for impersonating a baby.

Then, on Donald's eleventh birthday, his parents took him to Loch Ness for a treat.

"A treat!" exclaimed Donald, ungratefully. "This isn't a treat. This is just a lot of cold water and a few trees."

"We might see the monster."

"The monster!" he scoffed. "I'll believe there's a monster when I see it."

At which point his mother sprang her trap.

She swooped on the dummy with a monkey wrench, twisted it out of his mouth and hurled it into the loch. Donald did not hesitate. He plunged into the icy water and dived down into the inky depths to find his yummy dummy. But when he got to the bottom, he saw a strange shape ahead of him. It looked like a dinosaur with car tyres stuck in its throat. As Donald swam closer he could see that it was Nessie, and sitting beside her was a tiny baby monster with Donald's dummy in its mouth. Nessie roared a fierce warning and Donald knew that he was beaten. He kicked hard for the surface.

"The dummy's gone," he said glumly, as he stood dripping on the bank. "There's a monster sucking it now."

Donald's parents danced a Highland Reel and clapped their hands with joy. Their son was cured!

But in this they had miscalculated, because although Donald had lost his dummy, his urge to suck was as strong as ever. On the way home he did something that made his parents' blood freeze, something he hadn't done since he was a tiny baby, something that rang a bell in a Pie Shop in Perth. He raised his hand to his chin, looked at his thumb, as if disturbing some long distant memory, and stuck it in his mouth.

Donald's father slammed on the brakes and slued across the road.

"No," he shouted. "Not the thumb!"

"Take it out now!" wailed his mother, "or the Pie Man will get you!"

"Who?" slurped Donald.

"He'll cut off your thumbs."

"Not if I'm sucking them he won't," mumbled the boy with the sucking power of a bull elephant. "This is dead delicious. I don't know why I haven't tried it before."

In their panic, Donald's parents turned the car round, hired scuba-diving equipment and plunged into Loch Ness to retrieve the dummy. Donald's father had to show Nessie's baby how to suck its toes before she'd let him take it. But when he gave the dummy to his son, his son said, "No thanks. Yuck! Thumbs for me from now on!" And that was the end of that.

Or should I say *him*?

That night Donald retired to bed early to suck his thumbs. He was rotating them in his mouth, exploring their different smells and shapes and tastes with his nose and tongue, when he heard a bicycle skid to a halt on the pavement outside. There was a ping of a bell as someone dismounted, then a click of the front gate and footsteps on the path. Donald jumped out of bed and ran to the window. He nudged open the curtains and peered out through the crack. A shiny, black baker's bicycle was leaning on the lamppost outside and a waft of wholesome, savoury cooking drifted in through Donald's open window. The doorbell rang. He heard his parents open the front door and caught a snatch of the distant conversation.

"Pies?" said the voice of the stranger.

"Go away!" screamed his mother. And the front door slammed.

Donald watched the stranger step back on to the front path. He was wearing blue checked trousers, a black leather belt with a meat cleaver tucked inside, and a white chef's coat and hat. He was carrying a flat basket on his arm, laden with fresh, hot, steaming pies. He looked up at Donald's window, where Donald was sucking both thumbs together, and placed his basket on the ground.

Donald heard his parents running up the stairs.

"He's here!" they wailed. "Donald, wake up!"

"I am awake," he mumbled.

"Then open the door!" screamed his father.

"And don't suck your thumb!" howled his mother. "Or he'll chop it off!"

"I'm not sucking my thumb," he laughed, "I'm sucking my thumbs!"

Outside, the uninvited chef sat cross-legged on the finger of steam that snaked up from his hot pies, and rose magically towards Donald's window. He knocked on the glass. Donald slipped the latch with his nose and nudged the window open.

"You must be the Pie Man," he muttered with his mouth full.

"And you must be Donald," said the chef. "I hear you're a monumental sucker."

"I can suck out a sheep's eyeball at twenty paces," boasted Donald.

"Really?" said the Pie Man. "How useful." He clicked his fingers. A large circular pie dish leapt out of the basket on the front of his bike and flew up to the window.

On the landing, Donald's parents pleaded with their son to let them in.

"If you'd just like to place your thumbs on the dish," requested the floating Pie Man, sliding the cleaver from his belt. "I won't keep you any longer than I have to."

But Donald had not stopped sucking since the day he was born and he was not about to stop now! In fact he sucked his thumbs even harder so that the Pie Man couldn't have them. "You won't get them out," he said. "I can suck for ever." But this was not a wise tactic.

"So you want to play games?" said the Pie Man, smiling in a have-it-your-own-way way.

He grabbed Donald by the wrists and tried to tug the thumbs from his mouth, but they were stuck fast.

"See," sniggered Donald. "I win. You lose."

"There is more than one way to bake a pie," replied the Pie Man, mysteriously. Then he stopped tugging on the thumbs and with a flick and a twist he popped *all* of Donald into the dish.

"What are you doing?" squeaked the startled boy, as the Pie Man threw a roll of short-crust pastry over Donald's head.

"Today," he cackled, "I am baking Man Pie!"

When Donald's parents finally pushed open the door, Donald had gone. Sitting on the window ledge, however, was a hot, steaming, succulent pie with a hot, steaming, suck-a-thumb filling.

Bunny Boy

Harvest time is a most dangerous time to be out in the fields with eyes shut. At such a time it is advisable to pay close attention to the harvester's blades. As the countryman's saying goes:

Harvest time is a time of rebirth,
A time for Old Mother
To de-chaff the earth.
A time for blades to be whetted and honed,
For chopping and scything,
To reap what you've sown-ed.

Bill was a very naughty boy. He never ate his

greens, and because he never ate his greens he was sickly. He was frail and thin. He moved like a snail and had a pasty white skin like the underbelly of a dead fish. His hair was dry and wiry. His ears looked like two wrinkled walnuts. His teeth were loose and rattled in his mouth like a box full of dominoes. Bill hated greens even more than he hated the thought of his teeth falling out.

"Oh Bill," sighed his poor mother, who lived in a constant state of anxiety, "what are we going to do with you? If you don't eat your greens you'll never grow up into a big, strong boy."

"I don't care," said Bill. "I hate greens." Then he shuffled outside into the garden to meet a rabbit called Tubs.

Tubs was a fat rabbit who loved eating. He loved carrots and onions and artichokes, of course, but what sent his head into a spin and his ears into a flap were greens. Anything green in fact – cabbage, sprouts, lettuce, leeks . . . you name it. If it was green Tubs gobbled it up – stalk, leaves, heart and all.

Tubs Rabbit was the original Greedy Green Machine.

Now Tubs and Bill had something in common – Bill's mother's vegetable patch. On Bill's first birthday she had decided that the only way to get him to eat his greens was to grow them fresh in the garden. But Bill didn't care if the greens were fresh or frozen. He didn't care if she grew the biggest, plumpest green vegetables the world had ever seen, he was never eating them! Which was where Tubs came in. The deal between the skinny boy with rattly teeth and the plump rabbit with a well-oiled coat was so simple it was stupid. Tubs would eat what Bill wouldn't.

Every night, Bill left the garden gate open so that Tubs could sneak in and gobble greens till he burst. And every morning Bill's mother came out to tend her garden, threw her hands in the air and wept.

"Oh that wicked rabbit," she wailed. "That bad bad bunny! He's eaten all my green vegetables again. Now, there's nothing left for Bill."

"Oh, boo hoo!" sniggered Bill, who was watching from behind the potting shed. "I don't think I'll *ever* stop crying!"

Bill's mother waged war on the rabbit. She fired flat, stinging pebbles at his white tail with a catapult, until Bill had the bright idea of painting the tail green so she couldn't see it. She built an electric fence around the vegetables, but Bill air-lifted Tubs into the garden in a remote-controlled helicopter. She even buried rabbit traps in the lawn, but Bill (with the help of a bottle of tomato ketchup) pretended to get his finger horribly mashed in one, so she dug them all up.

Bill and Tubs were a team. Two halves of a whole. Each one making sure that the other got what he wanted, and in this respect they were like brothers.

Then one night, instead of going to bed, Bill's mother took a torch and shotgun down to her vegetable patch and kept guard till dawn. Bill could not get past her to leave the gate open and Tubs could not get into the garden to eat his greens. That night, untouched by rabbit teeth, the vegetables grew. In the morning Bill's mother proudly cut a huge cabbage and wheelbarrowed it inside for lunch. Bill felt sick when he saw it sitting on the kitchen table, so big and round and poisonously green!

Then he had an idea. While she was out of the room he painted the cabbage to look like a football and hid it under the stairs. But when his mother opened the cupboard door to get the lead to take the dog for a walk, the dog saw the ball and grabbed it in its mouth. Sadly the paint was still wet and his black nose turned white.

"You *will* eat cabbage for supper," his mother barked as she rinsed off the paint and the dog spit, returned the cabbage to the kitchen table and left the room. Bill didn't waste a second. He leapt outside, buried the cabbage in the garden and knocked in a sign on top of it.

DANGER! UNEXPLODED BOMB
DO NOT DIG UP

But he stupidly forgot to wipe the mud off his shoes when he came back in. "I know what you're up to," said his mother as she dug up the unexploded cabbage, "but it won't work." Then she washed off the worms and put the cabbage back on the table.

Bill would have to be more cunning still. He phoned the police and told them a gruesome tale about finding a severed head in a plastic bag. He asked them if they wanted to come and take it away for forensic evidence? Well, of course they did! But they brought it straight back when they discovered that the head had no hair, no ears, no nose, no lips and bore a striking resemblance to a cabbage.

When his mother had scraped off the putrefied garbage gunk, she said, "I'll have you know, young man, that I'm not as green as I'm cabbage-looking!" A puzzling phrase, which left Bill wondering if his mother wasn't human after all, and was in fact made from genetically modified vegetable matter.

Speculation aside, Bill quickly realized that there was only one way to get rid of this cabbage. Tubs would have to eat it. Tucking it under his anorak, Bill jumped on his bike, cycled through the gate at the bottom of the garden and pedalled across the cornfield towards his friend's burrow. Harmless enough you might think, until you remember that it was harvest time. Those harvesters' blades were whetted and sharpened. And Bill was a malnourished mouse of a boy, whose weedy legs could barely turn the pedals on his bike, let alone accelerate him out of harm's way in an emergency.

Tubs smelled the cabbage in Bill's anorak. He hopped out of his hole and bounced across the cornfield to meet the smell. Meanwhile, Bill cycled slowly towards Tubs. His underpowered bicycle wobbled in the ruts of dried earth. But (and this is the important bit) neither Bill nor Tubs could see the other over the tall, willowy wall of corn. It was just bad luck. A case of wrong time, wrong place.

Farmer Popple turned off the road and scraped his combine harvester through the wooden gate that led into the field. He was listening to the radio as he lowered the sharp, red blades to cut the corn. At the same time, puny Bill was suffering from a sudden attack of pedal fatigue and had fallen asleep in his saddle, and Tubs, being the fat, greedy green-guzzler that he was, had closed his eyes to dream about the delicious crunchiness of the upcoming cabbage. Both were still moving forward, but neither could see where he was going. Added to which, Farmer Popple fancied he had the voice of a rock star and closed *his* eyes to sing along with the radio. He was singing so loudly that he couldn't hear the roar of the engine or the swish of the blades as they sliced through the ears of corn.

Bill and Tubs only opened their eyes when the cold shadow blocked out the sun, but by then it was too late. The boy, the rabbit and the combine harvester came together on a knife edge, with a splittery-splattery, mishery-mashery, slip slop sliver of a slice up!

When Bill woke up in hospital there was a doctor standing over his bed.

"Hello Bill," he smiled. "How are you feeling?"

"What happened?" asked Bill.

"You had a little accident," said the doctor, "but the operation has been a complete success."

"There were bits of you all over the field," added the student nurse. The doctor put his hand over her mouth.

"But every last bit is stitched back," he said with false jollity. "And in the right place too, I hope!"

"Where's Tubs?"

"Who?" said the doctor.

"My rabbit friend," said Bill. The doctor looked uneasy as he turned away.

"You can go home tomorrow," he said.

"Where's Tubs?" repeated Bill as the doctor left the room. But nobody would tell him.

The next day, Bill went home. For the first time in his life, his mother did not make him eat his greens. The accident had softened her resolve. She just wanted him to get better. It came as something of a surprise, therefore, when Bill leant across the table and *helped himself* to a spoonful of sprouts.

"What are you doing?" she gasped.

"I don't know," said Bill, staring at the green-stuff on his plate. "I feel like a sprout. What's happening to me?"

"Maybe you've learnt your lesson," beamed his mother. "Maybe the accident has cured you!" Bill stabbed a sprout with his fork and popped it into his mouth.

"Delicious," he mumbled as he chewed it slowly. "Is there any more?"

"There's a whole vegetable patch!" she clapped. "Oh Bill, I'm so happy! Now that you're eating your greens you'll get stronger by the day!"

"Do you know what became of Tubs?" he asked suddenly. His mother put her hand on his shoulder.

"He was killed," she said softly. "I'm sorry Bill, but the doctor said he didn't feel a thing."

"Killed!" Bill gasped with shock.

"Sliced up slimmer than a wet peach," said his mother. "More sprouts?"

Bill was too upset to eat pudding. He went straight to bed and passed a fitful night dreaming weird dreams about huge rabbits with human feet noshing greens from his mother's vegetable patch. When he woke in the morning he had soil inside his mouth and fertilizer underneath his fingernails.

His mother was crying when he went downstairs for breakfast.

"What's wrong?" asked Bill, brushing the hair out of his eyes.

"It happened again last night!" she wailed.

"What did?"

"Another rabbit got into my vegetable patch and ate all my greens!"

"Really?" mumbled Bill, running his tongue across his gritty teeth.

"And it was a big one with clumping great feet and huge jaws..." Bill's mother stopped in the middle of her sentence and stared in disbelief at her son. "What have you done to yourself?" she asked.

"Nothing," he said. "Why?"

"You're fatter," she said.

"Probably those sprouts," said Bill.

"Are you fatter, Bill?"

"I feel fatter," he replied, "but I think it's just that my pyjamas are too small." Bill's mother was bamboozled.

"I did tell you that eating your greens would make you big and strong," she said, "but I never believed it could happen so quickly!"

It didn't stop there. Every night for the next week, Bill had the same dream about the huge rabbit raiding his mother's vegetables, and every morning he woke up to find that he was fatter. Not only that, but his hair had grown softer, his ears had grown pinker, his teeth had grown stronger, his nose had grown wetter, and his feet had grown longer than clowns' boots. But the day that Bill jumped out of his bath and rushed downstairs to show his mother his fluffy white tail, was the day that the doctor was called.

It was the same doctor who had operated on Bill in hospital.

"Oh dear," he said, turning as white as a sheet. "I never expected this to happen."

"What to happen?" said Bill's mother, as Bill wiped his wet nose on her apron.

"I never expected the rabbit to take over."

"What are you talking about?" she frowned. "Bill will you stop that! I'm trying to talk to the doctor!" Bill was hopping over the sofa and chairs and banging his head on the ceiling.

"After the accident with the combine harvester," the doctor explained, "Bill and Tubs were chopped into so many different pieces that it was hard to tell which bit belonged to whom. I just used what I could find to put Bill back together again."

"You mean bits of him aren't Bill at all?" squealed Bill's mother. "You mean bits of him are Tubs!" Bill knocked the kitchen door off its hinges with a sharp kick of his huge feet. "So that's why he's suddenly eating his greens!"

The doctor nodded with shame.

"Nnnaaa, what's up, Doc?" squeaked Bill in a strange nasal voice, grinding his long front teeth on the end of his chin.

"You've got to turn him back!" shouted Bill's mother.

"I can't," said the doctor, as Bill twitched his

nose and bounced out of the back door into the garden.

"But he's my son!" she cried.

"Not any more," the doctor said, as Bill began to dig himself a burrow. "I'm afraid that Bill is now a rabbit!"

From then on Bill's mother only ever saw her son at night. She hid behind a bush in the garden and watched his furry face and long strong teeth chomp their way through her vegetables. And every night, when Bill heard her sob for the loss of her only son, he wondered why she was so sad. After all, wasn't he doing what she'd always wanted? Wasn't he eating his greens?

Spit

Once upon a time a dirty boy spat on the pavement. What he didn't know was that the world was not as he thought and the pavement wasn't a pavement at all. It was the shoes of a very smart giant. His best shoes in fact. His crocodile-skin shoes. And when the giant saw the boy's disgusting spit on his best shoes he blew his top and gave the boy a mouthful. And believe me, when you've had a mouthful from a giant you never forget it.

The boy is still trying to dig himself out.

Superstitious Nonsense

Superstitious people are easy to spot. It's the person wearing a sou'wester on a sunny day, the joker juggling liver in the butchers, or the whacko throwing pepper at a passing red car. It's the man with boiled eggs in his pockets, the old lady with her school satchel on her back or the child with a shoe taped to either ear. They are life's little fruitcakes – scared of the unknown, living their lives by imaginary rules that no one else can understand.

If you are one of these people who believes in mumbo-jumbo, take care. For this is a tale of a girl driven mad by her superstitious mind. It could happen to you.

216

Penelope Jane changed her name by deed poll. She did it because Jane meant "pie-shoveller" in Gaelic, but more importantly because she wanted a name that meant "Oh beautiful conductor of the natural energy that flows from Mother Earth's bosom." She chose Pylon, which means "A tall structure erected as a support for electric power cables". As to the sanity of anyone who would change her name from Penelope Jane to Pylon, I leave you to be the judge.

Pylon lived with her dull parents, Mr and Mrs Gaslamp, in a dull little house with net curtains, a garage, and a sign on the front gate that said:

Beware of the
Monkey-men from Mars.
Do not pass this gate whistling
"Yes, I Have No Bananas!"
or they will invade!

Her life was ruled by stupid superstitions. Her barking brain had a list of dos and don'ts that would have kept a mind-doctor busy for a lifetime. For example, she had to get out of bed on the left or she'd start off the day on the wrong foot. She always had to open the back door during breakfast so that the Devil could leave and wouldn't be tempted to sit down for tea and crumpets. She always shook hands with the postman to ensure that her letters only contained good news, and if she had hiccups she had to rush around town to find a bearded policeman to give her a kiss.

Mr and Mrs Gaslamp were old-fashioned folk, simple and humdrum. They believed in an honest day's work for an honest day's pay, in clean socks and simple minds that called a spade a spade. Mr Gaslamp had a wooden leg as a result of a freak accident with a high-pressure hose and a chip buttie. Mrs Gaslamp had lost her hair in a window-cleaning cradle and was plagued by her nerves. They were the unluckiest pair alive, which was why Pylon had become so obsessed with superstitious non-sense in the first place.

Silly little things were blown up into whop-ping great issues that tore the family apart.

"I can't go on holiday!" Pylon whined with her flat, Northern vowels.

"But the bus is waiting!" pleaded her father. "We've been saving for this holiday for seven years!"

"But I can't get on *that* bus!"

"Why not, Pylon, dear?" Her mother had her best hat on. "It's a lovely bus and it's going to be a lovely holiday."

"It's number seventy-minus-ten 3," said the superstitious lump. She couldn't speak the word six. "Five plus one is my unlucky number."

"I'll have a word," said her dad, and he got the driver to change the number to 73.

"Now we can go on holiday!" her mum beamed.

"Oh no, not now," said Pylon. "Didn't you know? If you raise your voice during the first ninety minutes of the only holiday you've had in seven years, you'll be eaten by sharks."

"But nobody gets eaten by sharks in Birmingham!"

"There's always a first time."

"And who raised their voice?!"

"You did. Just now," said the obstinate girl, as she picked up her bags and hopped home. "Mind the cracks!" she shouted back at her mother, who was sitting on her suitcase weeping. "In the pavement, I mean. Don't want to be mauled by bears!"

Life with the Gaslamps was pretty much constant misery. Pylon was a purveyor of gloom and doom.

"None of us can know what's just around the corner," she said.

"It's that new supermarket, isn't it?" replied Mrs Gaslamp.

"I wish it *was* a laughing matter, mother, but it isn't. Precautions must be taken! When you're dressing, *don't* pull your shirt on before your trousers or you'll get ants in your pants. *Don't* pass a fish slice to the left or prawns will spit in your paella. *Don't* wash your hair if you've just met a monk or you'll go bald. *Don't* speak ill of the Royal Family or your head will be chopped off. *Don't* close your eyes when you're walking across a zebra crossing or you might get hit by a car."

Her mother chuckled. "I touch your father's wooden leg every morning," she said, "just to be on the safe side."

But Pylon was not amused. "*Never* sleep in a draught or every good idea you've ever had will blow away. *Never* take grass home on your shoe or geese will nest in your bathroom. *Never* leave a hamster in the same room as a cat."

"Why?" asked her mother.

"Why!" exploded Pylon. "Isn't that obvious? The cat'll eat it!"

It was just an ordinary day and Pylon's parents were doing a spot of gardening. An alder tree had sprouted in the middle of a dog rose, and its roots were entwined with deadly nightshade. Mr Gaslamp thought it made the flowerbed look crowded.

"It's like Brighton Beach," he joked, when it looked nothing like it. "I'm going to pull it out."

But as he did so, Pylon skipped into the garden. She was reciting the alphabet backwards to keep her dress clean, and was eating worms from a jar to stop her skin from wrinkling, when she saw her father take a grip of the alder stem near to where the roots were.

"No!" she shouted, choking on a fat worm. "You have to say sorry!" But her cry came too late. Her father tugged up the tree without so much as an "excuse me" and Pylon's face drained of colour.

"What's the matter?" her mother asked.

"An alder is a witch's tree! If you don't apologize when you pull it up, death and destruction will fall upon the house of Gaslamp. There's going to be a plague of frogs. We're all going to die!"

"Calm down," said her father. "It's only a bit of wood."

But Pylon meant what she said. She was utterly convinced that her father's stupidity had condemned her to an early grave!

From that moment on, she hated her parents. She thought they were laughing at her superstitions and trivializing her anxieties. She thought they *wanted* her to suffer bad luck. And because of this muddled thinking she went loopy, and wanted *them* to suffer bad luck instead. To this end, she decided to divorce them and take all their things.

The very next day, she set about her task. She read a book in the library, called "LAW FOR UNDER-ELEVENS". It told her that to be granted a divorce from her parents she would need to satisfy three conditions:

1) She should be more worldly-wise and to this end should see more of the world.
2) She should behave more like an adult and to this end should stop going to school.
3) She should have enough money to go shopping without her mother.

"Why haven't you done your homework?" her mother asked that night.

"I can't do homework any more," said Pylon. "Haven't you heard the saying – *Don't* do homework or a vampire bat will suck out all your blood?"

"Oh dear!" cried her gullible mother.

"It gets worse," lied the scheming girl. "Don't go to school while the teachers are there or they'll send you mad."

"No," gasped Mrs Gaslamp. "Says who?"

"Says everyone," said Pylon. "You have to be mad to go to school nowadays. And I'm not! So I shan't be going any more. I thought I'd travel the world instead, meet interesting people and visit exotic places."

"But we can barely afford to go to Birmingham," pointed out her father.

"*You're* not coming," said Pylon. "And I shall be paying for myself."

"But you're only ten," he said, "and you don't work."

"Not a problem," she smiled. "Ask and ye shall be given."

"Meaning?"

"Meaning I shall be paying for my trip around the world with my pocket money." Her parents exchanged deeply puzzled looks.

"But how?" they said. "You only get one pound a week!"

"Did!" she said, quietly. "To quote the famous words of Saint Denaceus Menaceus – if parents don't increase their child's pocket money by a lot, men with big sticks will beat them up!"

Mr and Mrs Gaslamp gave Pylon all the money they had in the bank and she went off around the world. And a very nice time she had too. She bought lots of clothes and when she came back she felt strong enough to leave her parents for good. But first, she needed somewhere to live.

"We've got a problem," she said. "When I was in Peru, an old lady warned me of an ancient Inca superstition – if parents do not give their house and everything in it to their daughter before she is eleven, the evil screaming will descend upon the girl like a fever, and she will scream and scream until she is sick. And then she will scream some more and won't be able to stop."

"Why?" frowned her father, who had recently been forced to sell his wooden leg to buy a can of tuna for their tea.

"It's written in the Great Peruvian Ledger of Superstitions," said Pylon. "It's just one of those things."

"But can't you just *not* scream?"

"No," said his daughter. "It's superstition."

"But where will we go?" trembled her mother, whose skin was blotched with a nervous red rash.

"The garage."

"It's got a car in it."

"That's not my problem," said Pylon. "But know this – if you live in a car, you *will* go far. You might win the Lottery, you never know." So that night, with only one suitcase between them, Pylon's feeble-minded parents moved into the car, leaving Pylon to live in the house on her own.

Pylon liked living on her own. She could do as she pleased. She watched television shows about ghosts and the supernatural, took out a sub-scription to a magazine called HOGWASH WEEKLY, which kept her up to date with all the latest superstitions, dressed in purple and wore mirrored scarves in her hair. If her parents ever turned up at the door, shivering with cold or weak with hunger, she always had a ready answer.

"*Never* give firewood to a stranger or they will come back for more."

"But I'm your mother."

Then one day, Pylon's luck ran out. It was Friday 13th, and Friday 13th was the scariest day of the year. Pylon was in such a nervous fluster when she rushed out to buy lucky seaweed to hang around the door, and blessed pigs' trotters to soak in the bath, that she didn't notice when she knocked over the salt cellar. As she hopped to the shops, avoiding the cracks in the pavement, she heard a siren and thought it was a police car. But it wasn't. It was an ambulance and she should have held her collar till she'd seen a dog, but she didn't. And when she came home, she was so busy counting her keys to escape from the headless coachman that she didn't spot the ladder when she walked underneath it. Only when she saw the salt on the kitchen floor did she stop, rewind her memory and realize that she had just broken three super-huge superstitions in the space of ten minutes. Her life was in danger!

She dragged a metal box out of the attic and placed it in the middle of the lawn. Then she laid a ring of garlic around the outside, lit four candles at the four points of the compass, danced a jig singing "Keep Me Safe, Oh Great Nangoblin!", lit a twig of willow, stood on her head and winked at worms, ate three Shredded Wheat, chalked the head of a bird on the lid of the box, and ate a beetle.

"What are you doing?" asked her father, who'd been watching from the garage.

"Protecting myself from all evil spirits," panicked his superstitious daughter. "Once I'm inside that box I shall be safe."

"Really?" said her mother, trying to take an interest.

"I am protected by the Circle of Min and the Force of Ftang," gibbered Pylon.

"Very nice too, dear. Do you mind if I pop in the house and fetch a couple of biscuits while you're in the box?"

"If you must," said Pylon, "but beware! That house is cursed!" She leapt inside the box. "While I, on the other hand, am as snug as a bug in a rug!" And she closed the lid, feeling safe and secure from all the evil demons outside.

The fact that a cow fell out of the sky at all was an unusual event. That it should have scored a direct hit on Pylon's metal box was spooky. That Pylon should have been squashed to death was the final icing on the most bizarre cake ever baked.

Mr and Mrs Gaslamp moved back into the big house and put up a headstone on Pylon's grave. It read:

Here lies Penelope Jane,
Superstitiously insane.
Fought her demons, lost the battle,
Went out in a storm of cattle.
Hopefully she's gone for good
And won't be coming back. Touch wood.

Head in the Clouds

Once upon a time there was a boy who wandered around with his head in the clouds. His parents called him Butterfly Brain but we shall call him Brian.

Brian was a dreamer. He had a mind that opened gates and ran with its arms outstretched into fields of daisies. He had a mind that jumped into a spiralling wind and was sucked up into a funnel of deep blue sky. He had a mind that sailed through the clouds like a royal swan on a lapping lake of whipped cream. Which meant that Brian's mind was always full of fancies and never had space for the ordinary things in life like clothes, buses, mealtimes, toothpaste, money, keys, books, sport, family, bed, posters, homework, pets and sock puppets. It meant that Brian was forgetful – "Now have I eaten lunch or not?" And *that* said with tomato stains on the tip of his nose. It meant that Brian was prone to accidents – bumping into lampposts, walking off cliffs, dropping like a stone down manholes. It meant that Brian was a loser. He could lose anything. His school books, his parents, his baby sister's pushchair, his baby sister, his bearded dragons, his mother's purse, his father's glasses, three lemons, a football team, and once (it would take too long to explain) the Mont Blanc Tunnel.

Breakfast was the only time of the day that Brian's parents could be guaranteed to see their son. At suppertime, more often than not, he was lost, having jumped off the bus at the wrong stop, or gone to the zoo to watch the penguins eat fish, or popped up to Buckingham Palace to offer sweets to the soldiers in the funny hats.

Sometimes his parents would find him talking to the plants at the local garden centre, or sometimes he'd turn up in the park, lying on his back watching wasps hover and hum like helicopters. It was easier, therefore, to make breakfast a time for the family, a time for Brian's parents to urge their absent-minded son to pull his socks up.

"Whose turn was it to feed the dog last night?" barked his mother. Brian looked around the table for the culprit, while the rest of the family looked straight at him.

"Me?! But I fed the dog last . . . erm. . ." He couldn't remember when he'd last fed the dog. In fact he couldn't remember a dog. Did they have one?

"And who had the last bath last night?" Brian could remember running a bath at some point in his life, but last night? It was all a bit hazy. He sniffed his forearm, but there was no smell of soap.

"It might have been me," he said. "I remember shining a torch through my skin, last night, to turn my fingers pink, but a bath. . ."

"Do you remember the flood in the hall?" twitched his tight-lipped father.

"I remember wet feet," said Brian. "I remember a yellow duck on the stairs." He smiled broadly. "Was it a real duck, do you think? Do ducks come in plastic?"

"I do wish you'd concentrate!" cried his mother. "You're a danger to yourself. You wander around all day with your head in the clouds. One day, Brian, you'll *lose* your head and not notice!"

"You left the taps on," explained his father. "Does any of this ring a bell?" But Brian's mind had drifted off into flights of fancy.

"Does anyone here know how many layers of biscuit it takes to make an ice-cream wafer?"

"Why do you ask?" his mother groaned.

"I was just thinking," he mused, spreading shoe polish on his toast and heaping three tablespoons of flour into his cup of hot water. "If a wafer was a magic carpet, how many times would it go round the world before it disintegrated?"

"Time for school," said his father, shaking his head.

"Does that mean me?" inquired Brian.

"You *do* go to school, Brian, yes."

"Just checking," said the boy. "Yesterday I forgot, and turned up for work in a car garage. They were very nice, but didn't have a pair of overalls small enough to fit me." Brian stood up from the table and picked his rucksack off the floor. "Ready!" he cried. But he didn't have his trousers on.

That same day after school, his head chock-a-block with bright ideas on how to train snails for Formula One Snail Racing, Brian turned right instead of left and kept on walking. When he stopped he was lost. He was standing on top of a hill, overlooking a deep valley carpeted by a thick, green wood. Two red kites wheeled against the sky and caught Brian's eye. As he watched them circle lazily, a strong wind whipped up from nowhere. The kites bumped up and down in the turbulence and swooped into the wood as the wind bowed the trees and flapped Brian's jacket like a small pair of wings.

Brian closed his eyes and imagined that he

too was flying. The clouds brushed past his face like puffballs. The earth turned miles below, peppered with dots of sheep and churches you could pop in your pocket.

Brian was running down the hill. Arms spread-eagled, out of control, slipping, sliding, with no thought for his own safety, when suddenly, a freak gust of wind stormed the hilltop at three hundred kilometres an hour. It bent the trees over like paper clips. It snatched up rocks and pitched them like baseballs. It stopped Brian dead and flipped him backwards up the hill like a tiddlywink. He tried to stand up. He rolled on to his feet and leant horizontally into the wind. But this was a twister and twisters take no prisoners. A brutal crosswind struck him from the side like a left jab. With a sharp crack and a clinical rip, Brian's head was torn clean off his neck. Like a balloon snatched from a child's hand it was wrenched into the air, tugged up thirty metres and then blown across the valley towards the wood.

What a shocker!

Poor Brian wasn't sure what was happening. He could feel his feet on the ground and he knew where his body was, but his eyes and ears were somewhere else. His eyes and ears were spinning in a swirling world filled with leaves and broken twigs. He could see the tops of trees. He could see a stalled swallow. He could also see his own headless body standing on the hilltop with its hands on its hips. But only briefly, because suddenly his body disappeared behind a tree and a rush of cold air filled his mouth and stretched his voice and made his eyes water.

The first branch broke the head's fall. The second branch snapped. The head ricocheted down to the third, bouncing like a ball through outstretched hands, until at last, with a soft thud, it came to rest in a bed of spongy bracken.

Brian had lost his head. His mother had said he would. If he'd gone straight home after school none of this would have happened.

He pinched himself to check he wasn't still dreaming, but his stump of a neck told him that it was all horribly real. What was he going to do? How could he hunt for his head without eyes?

"I've got it!" yelped the mouth. "If I shout loud enough, Brian's body can follow my voice." But as well as being the mouth it was also the spokes-part for every other bit of the head. "What was that, ears?" it said. "You're down here too, so how will the body hear me if I shout? Good point." But in the absence of any better plan, it was one that the mouth chose to ignore. "Over here, Brian!" it yelled. "Down the hill. In the wood. Run, Brian, run! Find your lost head!"

As luck would have it, Brian had super-sensitive toe bones that quivered as they picked up the sound waves from his voice. His body *felt* the words as they resonated through his skeleton like a deep itch. His body stumbled down the hill towards the guiding voice while the eyes kept a careful watch. "Left, left, left a bit more. RIGHT! STOP! STOP! STOP! STOP!" Thwack! Sometimes Brian's toes didn't get the message. "Sorry!" said the mouth on behalf of the eyes. "That was a tree."

At last Brian's body found Brian's head in the bracken. It was a tearful reunion in which Brian's arms held Brian's head against Brian's shoulder and Brian's eyes wept Brian's tears down Brian's back.

"Now," said Brian's mouth to Brian's arms, "pop the head back on and we can all go home." But the head wouldn't stick to the neck. It just kept rolling off like a beach ball on a dead seal's nose. "We need help," said the mouth.

So tucking the head under its arm, Brian's body walked back into town and the eyes spied a place called the Body Shop. It had a small sign in the window:

Body repairs undertaken at reasonable prices. Full service for older models. We stock spare parts for all makes of Scandinavian, European, African, Australasian, American, Indian, Chinese and Caribbean bodies.
MOT – £25.

Then in smaller letters underneath it explained

that MOT was cheap heart surgery and stood for *Mending Old Tickers*.

"Good heavens," exclaimed the man behind the counter. He was wearing blue overalls and was wiping his bloody hands on a rag. "What happened to you?"

"I lost my head," said Brian's mouth. "And now it's making my arms ache." The man slipped the head out from under Brian's arm and inspected it by turning it round and round in his hands until the face was almost entirely green. "I think I'm going to be sick," it gulped.

"Sorry," said the man. "Just looking."

"Can you sew it back on?" asked Brian's mouth.

"I could try," said the body mechanic. "But there's something wrong inside. Mind if I take a look?"

"Be my guest."

The body mechanic placed Brian's head on a table, squatted down and gently inserted a long, cold, metal torch into the ear. Brian's body shivered.

"That tickles," said the mouth.

"Well I never," exclaimed the man suddenly. "I've never seen that before."

"What?"

"Your head's full of clouds! Look!"

The man gently tapped the back of Brian's head and three baby clouds puffed out of his mouth like smoke from a steam train. Brian's face was flabbergasted.

"So my parents were wrong," he gasped. "All these years, I haven't been walking around with my head in the clouds at all, I've been walking around with clouds in my head! Does that mean I don't have a brain?"

"It's difficult to see," said the body mechanic. "Are you forgetful?" Brian nodded, forgetting that his head was sitting on a table. It rolled over the edge and crunched to the floor.

"Ow!" wailed the mouth.

"Hmmmm," mumbled the man. "Listen, I can offer two cures. You can either go for a new head entirely and chuck this one out. . ." While he was speaking, he took three plastic containers off the shelf, removed their lids, unpacked the cotton wool padding and pulled out three heads. "These are spares I've had lying round for years," he said. "I've got a choirboy, a rugby player – bit of a broken nose on that one – or a Head Girl." He laughed. "That's about *all* she is these days."

"And the other choice?" asked Brian, who sang like a parrot, hated sport and looked positively stupid in a dress.

"I give the original head a good clean out," said the mechanic. "Blow those clouds away, put some glue on the bottom and you can have it back in an hour."

"That one," chose Brian, as the man pressed a red ticket and a silver key into his hand.

"Whatever you do, don't lose that ticket," he said. "It tells me which head is yours."

"And the silver key?" asked Brian's mouth.

"The key is irreplaceable. After any operation involving cloud extraction, there is always a small risk of nimbosity. The head must be packed in cotton wool, sealed in a metal container to protect it from cumulus vaporization and kept in the dark until the eyes open."

"Gosh," said the mouth, "And what happens if the box is opened *before* I've opened my eyes?" The mechanic looked stern.

"To avoid a *fatal* unlocking," he said meaningfully, "there is only ever one key. Lose it and your head will be locked in the box for ever. Do you understand?" Then he took a fan from a drawer and positioned it next to one of Brian's ears. "You can wait in the waiting room," he said to Brian's body. "I trust you can find your way without a head?"

"Of course it can," said Brian's mouth, as Brian's eyes watched Brian's body miss the open door and crack Brian's neck on the wall.

Now, just how easy is it to keep hold of a ticket and key for one hour? It's not hard if you've got hands and pockets, and Brian's body had both. But you must remember that this was Brian and Brian could lose anything.

Within seconds of entering the waiting room, he drifted off into a dream in which he imagined that he was in a cell. An attic cell in a tower – and that he was Rapunzel, and that down below was a handsome prince on a white charger, pleading with Rapunzel to toss down a lock of her hair so that he might climb up. What other lock did Brian have? With reckless abandon, he pulled the key out of his pocket and tossed it out of the window. And as he did so, a red ticket fluttered to the ground and slipped between the floorboards.

After the operation, the mechanic called Brian through. He was pleased to announce that he had successfully blown away the clouds and had found a brain underneath. It wasn't a terribly big one, but that came as no surprise to either of them. The man placed a metal box on the counter and asked for Brian's ticket.

"What ticket?" replied Brian's muffled voice. His head was packed in cotton wool inside the box.

"The ticket that tells me that the head inside this box is yours," said the man. Brian's body patted its pockets.

"I've lost it," he said. Then he added a little

desperately, "Surely you recognize me? I'm the boy with no head. I was in here a few minutes ago."

"How am I supposed to recognize you without a head?"

"That's because you've got it. Open the box. Look at my mouth. That's me talking."

"No can do!" said the mechanic. "Nobody can open the box until the eyes are open." Brian's shoulders slumped with despair and from inside the box came the sound of gentle sobbing. "Oh, all right!" said the mechanic, who was not a cruel man. "I'll make an exception just this once. Take it home." He pushed the metal box across the counter. "But remember to wait until your eyes are open, before you unlock it."

When Brian got home his parents took one look at him and burst out laughing.

"Good trick!" hooted his mother. "Have you hidden your head inside the collar of your shirt?"

"No, I've lost it," said Brian's muffled voice.

"Lost it!" gasped his parents.

"You always said I would if I didn't concentrate."

"But that was a joke," cried his father. "You can't lose your head. Where is it?"

"In this box," said their headless son. "I had the clouds removed. They found a brain."

"I can't think why," screeched his mother. "Get it out. Get it out, Brian, and we'll stick it back on!"

"But I can't," said Brian. "The mechanic said that I have to wait until. . ." His voice trailed off, because just then his eyes opened. His eyelashes rose on a cotton wool world. Brian flinched. Up close the cotton wool looked like clouds – white, fluffy, fleecy clouds.

"What's the matter?" asked his father.

"Why don't you open the box?" his mother shrieked.

"I can't," replied Brian's teeny-tiny voice. "I've lost the key as well."

Which meant that silly old Head-in-the-Clouds had his head in the clouds for ever.

When the Bed Bugs Bite

In a faraway place just between the Land of Dreams and the Valley of Nightmares, is a block of ice that spins through the Napasphere at twice the speed of light. Inside this block of ice is an answerphone, where all the goodnight wishes of the world are recorded and stored until they are listened to by an old lady with white hair, whose job it is to decide which ones should be granted.

Night night,
Sleep tight,
Don't let the bed bugs bite.
If they do,

Get a shoe,
And squash those nasty bugs in two!

Hannibal was every bit as bad as a bed bug. He was a nasty biting boy with little, sharp, pointed teeth like a piranha. Nine years of biting flesh and bone, and doors and ducks and cars and cousins and friendly dogs, had ground down the enamel into dental daggers of which Hannibal was unnaturally proud. He could not sit next door to another human being, be it friend or stranger, be it at a birthday party, in the cinema or on a park bench, and *not* lean across for a quick munch.

Hannibal adored the noise people made when he sank his teeth into their flesh – that high-pitched squeal of surprise as they leapt into the air. It was the only time he'd ever seen a teacher fly! Animals were less fun. Apart from anything else they tended to bite back, and they came in such extraordinary sizes! An elephant could take a big bum bite in its stride, but a big bum bite on a hamster generally ensured that there was only half a hamster left.

Inanimate objects that didn't squeal, such as pillows, tricycles and chair legs, were good for practice bites, but there was nothing quite as funny as the crunch of a straw hat on top of the head of a fat lady on a bus!

Hannibal's parents lived in fear of their son. Not so much because of the missing body parts – both had lost ear lobes and fingertips – but because Hannibal was a menace to society. He could clear a pavement in six seconds. When he walked down the High Street he left howling hordes of chewed pedestrians in his wake; mothers with molared ankles, nippers with nipped noses and gnawed nuns with teeth marks in their wimples. It goes without saying that his parents were embarrassed by their son's horrible habit.

"Do have a care, Hannibal," his father scolded, wagging his finger under his son's nose, "or one day you'll bite off more than you can chew."

"It's so unhygienic," added his mother. "People are uncooked, Hannibal! You don't know where they've been."

"Who cares?" he said, as his greedy eyes followed the raw finger.

"And another thing," said his father, "The headrest on the back of the seat in the car."

"What about it?" the boy asked innocently.

"Where is it?" Hannibal pointed to his stomach.

"Yum, yum." That wagging finger was starting to look tasty as well.

"And how are we going to pay for *this*?" wailed his mother, waving a piece of paper in the air. It was a bill from the Natural History Museum, for bone damage caused when Hannibal bit the Tyrannosaurus Rex.

"We're not," said Hannibal, snapping the paper into his mouth and swallowing it whole. Then his eyes swivelled left and his teeth snapped again.

"Yowwwwwwwww!" That was one less fingernail his father would have to trim.

Hannibal was sent to bed, where his parents wrenched the duvet from his clenched jaw and laid down the law.

"Curb your gnashing or else!" roared his father.

"But I'm good at it," grinned Hannibal wickedly, chomping the leather-patch paw off his teddy bear's arm. "And it's fun! Where are you going?" His parents were leaving the room. "You haven't done the night-night thing," he whined in a tiny, injured voice. "Night night, sleep tight, hope the bed bugs don't bite. . ."

"No," she interrupted. "Because it's not true."

"What's not true?" said Hannibal. His mother blushed and turned to her husband for help.

"We hope the bed bugs *do* bite," he said starkly.

"But that would hurt!" blurted the shocked boy.

"Yes, it would, wouldn't it? Your teeth have tried our patience to the bone," explained his father. "It is our wish to see you taught a lesson, Hannibal, and if that lesson is a serious biting from bed bugs then so be it." And with that, they left the room without giving their son so much as a goodnight kiss. The school of hard nips had taught them not to put temptation in tooth's way.

As they left the room, however, an answer-phone rang in a block of ice. In that faraway place just between the Land of Dreams and the Valley of Nightmares, a tape clicked on and a wrinkled white finger reached for a pencil. The goodnight wishes of the world were about to be granted.

That night, Hannibal slept fitfully as his father's angry words echoed through his head.

"Hope the bed bugs *do* bite. . .
Hope the bed bugs *do* bite. . .
Hope the bed bugs *do* bite. . ."

Weird dream-like pictures flittered behind his eyes. There was a huge black bug wearing a fluorescent cape and peaked crown, and carrying a long pole with a golden orb on the end. She was a Queen Bug. She was flying down a street full of zebras and children, and sniffing each child with her feelers. Occasionally she would stop and touch a child on the head with her orb, whereupon the child would disappear. And suddenly one of them was Hannibal. How *he* had got into this dream he didn't know. Only he wasn't on the street any more.

She touched his head with her orb and he found himself in his own bed. Only it *was* his bed and it *wasn't*. It was more like a cot, with bars, and he was trapped, and the Queen Bug had changed. She was shiny. Her shell had been polished. She was wearing rubber boots and hoovering around his bed, only her machine was blowing not sucking. She was filling his mattress with tiny sets of false teeth, which nipped and snapped and clickety clacked! And there was no escape, because of the bars, and she was dribbling! Hannibal was covered in a thick black paste that the Queen Bug was dribbling from her mouth! And the paste was setting off, hardening like papier-mâché! And Hannibal couldn't move! Not even his teeth!

"Night night," said the Queen Bug, "sleep *tight*!" Trussed up in his solid cocoon, looking like a black bug himself, Hannibal could do little else. Except scream!

Hannibal jerked awake. He was lying in his own bed, but there were no bars, no false teeth and no dribbling Queen Bug. It had just been a nightmare. Nothing had changed. Hannibal was still a biter.

The next day at break, he gnawed the neck of a new boy. In History, he got a splinter in the roof of his mouth from accidentally swallowing the blackboard rubber. At lunch, he polished off his plate (in all senses of the word), and when the headmistress hauled him out of maths and reached up to point out teeth marks on the school trophies, he couldn't help himself – he did to her bum what he'd done to countless elephants before. You should have heard the scream!

"You horrible brute of a boy," she wailed. "Go home! Go home now and don't come back until you have changed beyond all recognition!" And then, even though she knew she shouldn't do it, she propelled him out of the school with a hefty hoof up the bottom.

On the way home, however, Hannibal noticed the first change. His teeth developed a life of their own. They started to itch. He tried to scratch them, but his nails failed. So he clamped his jaws together and tried to *squeeze* the itch out of the nerve endings, but this just made matters worse. His teeth went haywire. They bit a pit-bull terrier, snapped at a tourist, snaffled ice-cream from a pushchair, stripped a wing mirror from a car, chomped on a Chinese delivery boy, snacked on a semi-detached garden gnome and munched a chunk from a lollipop lady's lollipop. She was an old black lady wearing a fluorescent coat and a flat-topped cap. Her back was stooped and her head appeared to be fused to her shoulders so that when she turned round she had to twist from the waist. She seemed strangely familiar, in a dreamy sort of way.

Hannibal had just bitten the yellow "*Stop Children*" sign on the end of her pole and was running towards the opposite pavement when he heard a sinister rattling noise behind him. He stopped and turned to see what it was, but before he was halfway round there was a sudden screech of brakes and a loud blast on a horn. The lollipop lady was standing in the path of an oncoming truck. Her shoulders spun round. Her jaw gaped. Her eyes stuck out like organ stops. She tried to spring across to the pavement, but her old joints were rusty.

Hannibal gasped in horror as the truck hit her full on and tossed her into the air. Then everything went silent until she landed with a sickening crunch on the tarmac. He expected her to explode, but she didn't. She bounced. Twice – once on to her back and once back on to her feet. Then she brushed herself down and hissed, "My fault. No damage. But I fear there may be to your truck." She was right. The truck's bonnet was crushed to a pulp. She must have had strong bones.

And still Hannibal did not recognize her. Not even when she turned to face him. Not even when her hat jiggled on her head and two twitching feelers flopped out from underneath the brim. Not even when she leant forward and touched him on the head with her golden lollipop.

Hannibal did not know it, but he had just been chosen. His parents' bedtime wish was about to come true.

That evening, during supper, the doorbell rang and Hannibal leapt up to bite the stranger at the door. When he opened the door, however, biting became impossible. His jaw was too slack from gawping. Outside was a woman dressed in a black rubber body suit, black rubber cape and black motorcycle helmet.

"Have no fear, the Bug Exterminator's here!" she sang. "Excuse the garb, but it stops creepy-crawlies sneaking up my trouser legs."

"Are you a bug?" asked Hannibal. "You look like one."

"Would I exterminate them if I was?" she laughed, trying to hide a faint rattle in her throat. "Now then I've been told there are bed bugs in your bedroom."

"Really?" said Hannibal.

"Yes, *really*!" she said tetchily. "Why else would you beg them not to bite you?"

"I thought that rhyme was just a bit of nonsense."

"Then it's time you opened your eyes," she said, as she picked up the stainless steel cylinder by her feet and stepped inside. She was wearing wellington boots. Smoke drifted lazily from the cylinder's lid and droplets of water beaded its surface.

"What's that?" he asked.

"My vacuum cleaner," she replied, "for sucking up bugs when I find them." There was a tiny scuttling noise inside the chamber like miniature mice scratching sandpaper.

"And are those bed bugs I can hear inside now?" he said.

"Where's your bedroom?" she replied, ignoring the question.

Hannibal's parents were locked out. Only Hannibal was allowed in the bedroom with her. She wanted to know exactly how he slept – on his left, on his right, on his front, on his back, in a ball, flat out like a plank, or upside down like a fruit bat? Then, when he had told her, she stuck the nozzle of her vacuum cleaner under his bedclothes and switched the machine on.

"Are you sucking the bed bugs out?" he enquired.

"Something like that," she replied, evasively. For two or three minutes the cylinder made a noise like gravel rattling in a tin, then there was a loud pop and she switched the sucker off. The scuttling noise inside the metal cylinder had disappeared.

"That should do it," said the Bug Exterminator. "Mission accomplished! I'll let myself out. Night night. Sleep *tight*. . ." And there she left it, her unsettling laugh drifting down the stairs as she scuttled away into the night.

An hour later, as Hannibal hazily drifted in and out of sleep, he saw what he thought were tiny footprints on his duvet. Surely just a trick of the light. He pushed his feet further down the bed into a pocket of cold air and wriggled his toes. It was like waving a red rag to a bull. The bed bugs waited for his first snore before scuttling out from their hiding place. Then they swarmed across his feet, ran up his legs and sank their tiny little teeth into his soft white flesh.

Hannibal did not wake up. He was having that nightmare again. Only this time the Queen Bug was wearing a black rubber body suit, a black rubber cape and a black motorcycle helmet. And when her feelers brushed Hannibal's skin, they felt *real*!

In the morning, Hannibal woke as normal and trotted into the bathroom. His eyes were half-closed as he brushed his teeth, but his arm felt stiff and his mouth felt tight, and when he got dressed his clothes split across his back, which was as smooth and heavy as pig iron.

When he went down to breakfast, his mother screamed and dropped the pan of scrambled eggs on the floor. She ran out of the kitchen howling like a baby and bumped into his father who took one look at his son and fainted. Hannibal finished his cereal with an un-characteristic slurp, shrugged his bulky shoulders and left the house for school.

As he walked down the road, he was conscious

that people were staring at him. Some crossed the road, others ran in the opposite direction, mothers covered their children's eyes and hit him with their handbags, and a rubbernecking driver drove his car into a postbox. It was all most peculiar. What had got into everyone this morning?

At school he found out. When he strolled into the playground his friends screamed and hid under benches.

"What's wrong?" he shouted, in a rattling voice he barely recognized as his own. "I won't bite." But of course nobody believed him.

The Headmistress came running out of her office with a face as white as pastry. "Hannibal!" she gasped. "When I said you could only come back once you'd changed beyond all recognition, this was *not* what I meant!"

"I don't understand," said the boy. "What do you mean?"

"Get me the exterminator!" she yelled, grabbing a mop from the janitor and poking Hannibal in the chest with it. "Keep back, you beast!" Hannibal was confused. Why did she need to call the exterminator? And why had she trapped him in a corner? And what on earth was that THING he could see reflected in the window?!

Hannibal crunched his jaws together with a grinding noise that sounded like a rasp file dragged across jagged metal. Staring back at him from the glass was not a boy, but a bug. A huge black bed bug with munching mandibles and flicking feelers! And in his head all that Hannibal could hear was the nonsense.

> *Night night,*
> *Sleep tight,*
> *Don't let the bed bugs bite.*
> *If they do,*
> *Get a shoe,*
> *And squash those nasty bugs in two!*

But now that *he* was a bed bug, didn't that mean. . .

Suddenly a motorbike roared into the playground, leaping the fence and screeching to a halt in a cloud of burning rubber.

"You again!" roared Hannibal, but the bug exterminator already knew that. And before Hannibal could move she whacked him with a giant shoe and split him down the middle like a pistachio nut.

In that faraway place, just between the Land of Dreams and the Valley of Nightmares, a wizened finger pressed a button marked ERASE and the answerphone tape rewound to the start. To begin again. To wait for the next goodnight wish.

Who knows, it may be yours.

The Decomposition of Delia Dethabridge

There are two lobes at the side of your brain that look like floppy saddlebags. They are full of all the knowledge that a human being acquires during his or her lifetime. At birth they are no bigger than peas, but when a person has reached the wise old age of eighty they are big and squidgy like lilos and press against the bones of the inner ear, which is why old people don't hear so well. Now obviously *some* people cram knowledge into their saddle bags until they're fit to burst and these people are called clever*clogs,* but other people hardly use their saddle bags at all, preferring to forego the gathering of knowledge in pursuit of ignorance, and these people are called *planks.*

Delia Dethabridge was a bit of both. She was a clever girl who did no work. She was an only child who had been raised by her academic parents (both dusty professors at Oxford University) to believe that she was the centre of the universe. As a result, she listened to nobody but herself.

At school she refused to do homework. She said she didn't need to and besides, homework interfered with her evening's entertainment. She was partial to couch-potato-ing in front of the telly, and when her teachers demanded an explanation she said, "I don't do homework, because it's a well-known fact that girls are much cleverer than boys and I'm the cleverest girl out of all the girls, so what's the point in doing stuff I already know?" which was horribly cocky and didn't make her a lot of friends. She knew it all (or so she told the world) and was horrible to those who didn't, mocking their mistakes and sneering at simple errors of memory.

"Don't you know anything, Alvin? Your saddlebags must be smaller than peanuts! If there's one thing us girls hate in boys it's ignorance. So that means you'll never have a girlfriend, never get married, never have children, and probably die all alone in a smelly old loft with pigeons and rats and no tiles on your roof!"

"I only said *Alfred* Einstein by mistake," protested Alvin. "I know his name's Albert really. It just slipped out."

"Oh sure!" Delia jeered. "Like your brain. Slipped out at birth. Pondlife!'

Delia thought boys were especially vile, because all they liked was football, which was rough and rude and played by boneheads who'd had all the sense knocked out of their skulls from heading the ball.

Spotty Tony Cronk was that stupid, thought Delia, he still couldn't tie his own shoelaces! "That's because I've broken my fingers!" Tony protested. "Huh!" she snorted haughtily. "Catching a ball, I bet!"

"Catching them in a fold-up seat at the Royal Ballet, actually."

"Ballet!" scoffed Delia. "Don't make me laugh! You couldn't tell a sugar-plum fairy from a plum duff!"

"Suit yourself!" said Tony. "At least I can tell who my friends are." Which was the truth. Delia Dethabridge may have been clever, but she didn't have any friends. Pupils didn't like her, because she belittled them, and teachers didn't like her because she never did her homework.

Then one day, her weak-jawed English teacher, Mr Pune, who had more in common with a limp lettuce than a human being, fell sick. He caught a nasty dose of green-fly off a rose bush and was advised to spend six weeks in bed – a flower-bed of course – and to take two shovels of manure three times a day.

A replacement teacher appeared in class. Her name was Ms Whetstone. She was fifty years old with a sharply hooked nose, a pointy chin, narrow lips, limbs as thin as pipe cleaners and wild, grey hair that tumbled over her neck like wire wool. She had a weird way of speaking.

She spat words across the room like darts. Words like *punishment* and *beating* and *punctual handing in of homework*. In Ms Whetstone's class there was nowhere to hide, as Delia soon found out.

"And where's your essay, Delia?"

"In my head," came the smug reply.

"I can't mark your head," said the teacher. "More's the pity."

"Then you'll just have to take it from me that it's excellent and unquestionably worth an A-star with knobs on."

Ms Whetstone narrowed her eyes and the class fell silent. "If I want to take anything from you, young lady," she hissed in a steely, soft voice, "I shall just take it. I don't need your permission."

Delia stared into the new teacher's eyes. They were perfectly still and as dark and deep as the barrel of a highwayman's flintlock.

"So, while the rest of the class reads, Delia, you will make a start on last night's homework."

"*Now?*" came the burst of indignation. "In the middle of a lesson?"

"Yes. I want to watch you doing it."

Delia scowled. "But I don't do homework. I'm far too clever. I'm a genius!"

"Then you'll have it finished in no time, won't you?" smiled Ms Whetstone. "Or maybe you'd like me to set you something harder?"

Steam rose from the back of Delia's collar, but words failed her.

"I didn't think so," smiled the new teacher. "You may start. A five hundred word composition entitled 'My Worst Nightmare'. Carry on."

But Delia folded her arms defiantly across her chest and sat back in her chair.

"I said," repeated Ms Whetstone, slowly licking her lips, "carry on."

The pouting girl gasped. The woman's tongue was red and forked like a snake's.

My Worst Nightmare
by
Delia Dethabridge

Because I am so clever, my worst nightmare

would have to be something like this. A beastlike something that comes in the middle of the night (when everything is dark and scary and fences crash like slap-sticks that Punch whacks Judy on the head with) and makes me stupid. *Because if you're stupid you can't read bus numbers and you think kicking someone is funny, whereas being brilliant like me is different. Being brilliant means I will one day be very rich and famous and probably on telly, on some celebrity game show or presenting* Top of the Pops. *Anyway, what is my worst nightmare was the question and here comes the answer. Being turned into a dumbo by a troll called Gormless. He would have a big face with warts and a scrubby beard and huge smelly feet, covered in mud, with toenails that hadn't been cleaned ever. And on his hands, long fingernails, like sharp pointed sticks. He is really ugly. He snatches me from my bed and takes me away to the Land of the Really Thick where I would scream things like, "Put me down!" and "Don't touch my brain. The world needs my intelligence!" And then the troll*

*would do something to me in a horrible way
and this would be it. . .*

That was when the bell rang for the end of
school. Delia stopped writing and closed her
book in the middle of the sentence.

"You will bring me that finished essay first
thing tomorrow," said Ms Whetstone, "or
there'll be trouble."

Delia snorted like a haughty horse that had
no intention of being ridden. "We'll see,"
she said.

"Oh, will we?" replied the surprised teacher.
"Just exactly who's threatening who here?"

"We'll find out tomorrow," said the
swaggering girl as she picked up her exercise
book and left the classroom. It seemed heavier
than usual and Delia had to use two hands to
carry it.

She did no work that night. She watched six
hours of television instead and left her exercise
book upstairs next to her bed, where she
wouldn't have to look at it. When she went to bed

she moved it on to the floor under the mattress, and was on the brink of going to sleep when Ms Whetstone's face popped into her mind.

"Stupid woman," she muttered. "What does she want now.?"

No sooner had Delia asked the question than she heard a noise. It was a shuffly sort of a noise, like a heavy sack being dragged across floorboards. And it was right underneath her! She bent over the side of her bed and peered upside down at the exercise book lying in a pool of blue light on the dusty floor

Suddenly the book twitched. Then it slid across the floor and instead of a shuffly noise there was a pig-like grunt and a rather unwholesome smell of cheesy feet. Delia held her nose and snatched up the book, only to find that the paper was covered in dirty footprints and across the two central pages a picture had appeared – that of a short, hideously ugly, lumpen-faced man with a beehive of hair. He had long fingernails sharpened to a point and a mouthful of broken teeth. Only it wasn't a normal picture, because *this* picture moved!

The squat little gremlin shook his fist at Delia and howled like a wee-widdly wolf. "Release me!" came his tiny cry. It was so distant that it made less noise than a metal nut bouncing on the track in the middle of a Grand Prix. But Delia heard it. "Write me to life!" She dropped the book. "Finish the story!"

With horror, Delia realized what was happening. This freakish figure was the troll of her creation. This was Gormless, and he was trapped in the story, because the story had no ending. The troll had nowhere to go. Which was *exactly* how Delia liked it. She was scared. She slammed the book shut and stuffed it into her rucksack, where the little, gruff voice of Gormless was muted by her gym socks.

The next morning, however, Ms Whetstone asked for Delia's completed essay.

"I couldn't finish it," said the girl.

"You mean you *didn't* finish it," corrected the teacher. There's a difference, Delia. One is excusable, the other is not."

"No, I couldn't finish it," protested the girl,

who for once felt she had a genuine excuse, "because it was about a troll called Gormless who made people stupid, but he came alive in my book and I was scared that if I finished the story I would release him from the pages and he would eat me."

"And you honestly expect me to believe that?" screeched the bony teacher.

"But it's the truth," Delia said sheepishly, even though she knew that it did sound a bit far-fetched.

Ms Whetstone suddenly snapped. With a vicious voice that ripped through the room like bolts of lightning, she cried, "You have been lying to me, Delia! Because of that you will now open your exercise book and finish your essay by the end of this lesson!"

Even Delia was cowed by the ferocity of the teacher's voice. She didn't want to do it, but she had no choice. Slowly, nervously, with a hand that trembled like a dragonfly's wings, she opened her book and turned to the page where she'd written her story. And there he was. The troll!

Delia had less than thirty minutes to come up with a plan to save her skin. If this troll came off the page he would turn her into a pea-brain, and if she was a pea-brain, all the other children would tease her and call her names like "Dullia Dethabridge" and "She Who's As Thick As Elk's Dung." Then suddenly she had it. It was *her* story. *She* was writing it. *Her* pen made the troll what it was. It didn't have to be a nasty beast. If she wrote a happy ending, the troll could be a jolly soul with sweet-smelling feet!

She scratched out the word horrible and substituted a more friendly word instead.

And then the troll would do something to me in an unexpectedly kind and gentle way and this would be it . . .

He would give me a kiss and say he was a fairy troll with the power to grant me three wishes, which I must make instantly to make my life happy and wealthy. So I ask for world fame, a million pounds and the new Boys 'R' Us single, which the nice troll grants. And that

is my worst nightmare – that this friendly *troll*
will one day go away.

Delia put down her pen and sighed with relief.
Turning the frightening troll into a harmless
friend was the work of a genius, but then Delia
already knew what she was, didn't she! Even if
the troll did come to life now, she wouldn't
have to be scared. She lifted up the page to see
if the troll had turned into a nicer-looking
creature with soft skin and long blonde hair
like a Viking warrior, but he wasn't there. His
image had vanished, along with the smell of
his cheesy feet.

When the bell rang, Delia got up from her desk
and handed her book in to Ms Whetstone.

"Good," said the teacher. "You've finished.
Wait a moment." She raised her hand to stop
Delia from leaving. "Stand there till I've
marked it."

Delia watched the teacher frown as she read
through the composition. "Is there anything
wrong?" she asked.

"Well, yes, there is," said the teacher. "I'm afraid the ending doesn't work."

"Yes, it does," said Delia. "It works brilliantly. It kept the troll inside the book."

"I meant as a piece of creative writing, Delia. You can't describe a troll as being nasty at the top and then make him nice at the end. The two halves don't join up."

Delia didn't like the sound of this. She wasn't sure what was coming next, but she had a pretty shrewd idea.

"What do you mean?" she asked nervously.

"I mean that the ending must be rewritten," said Ms Whetstone.

"No!" squeaked Delia. "No, that's not a good idea. In fact that's the worst idea I've ever heard in my life. I won't do it!"

"But you don't have to, my dear," Ms Whetstone smiled. It was a funny lopsided smile, which suggested that she was moderately unhinged. "I'm going to write it for you." And then she laughed for the first and only time in her life, while Delia turned as white as a corpse and fainted.

276

Nobody quite knows what happened to Delia Dethabridge that night, but suffice it to say that she went home as clever as she'd ever been and returned the next morning as dim as a five-watt bulb in a blackout. She never regained her cleverness. She failed all her exams and ended up licking batteries for a living to see if they were dead or not. But every cloud has a silver lining. She never teased others for being stupid again. How could she? There was nobody in the whole universe who was quite as stupid as she was!

In case you're a detective and fancy a bit of a puzzle, they do say that the key to what happened in Delia's bedroom on that fateful night lies within the following passage, penned by Ms Whetstone as a conclusion to Delia's story. I can't work it out. Maybe you can.

He snatches me from my bed and takes me away to the Land Of The Really Thick where I would scream things like, "Put me down!" and "Don't touch my brain. The world needs my intelligence!" And then the troll would do something to me in a horrible way and this would be it. . .

The troll takes me out of bed and stands me in the moonlight so he can see better. Then he pushes his long fingernails into my earholes and bursts the saddlebags of knowledge on the sides of my brain. It's like a butcher's hook punching a hole in a big bag of sawdust. The knowledge spills out. It pours out of my ears until there's nothing left in the saddlebags but air. From being a know-all, suddenly I'm a know-nothing. And that's the way it stays, because the troll eats my knowledge and goes away to write the Encyclopaedia Britannica.

The End

Delia Dethabridge
(with a little help from a fiend)

The Grass Monkey

The boy's name was Spike. Spike, because he was born with a spike of hair in the middle of his head, like a clump of grass in a desert. He was a spindly runt of a child. Thin gangly limbs, long feet and a big head with sticky-out ears like a monkey's. He was ten years old and lived with his sick mother in a caravan, on a piece of unwanted concrete underneath a flyover. They were very poor. Apart from the caravan, all they owned in the world was a bony cow called Ruby. They had bought her for her milk, but since she had no grass to eat, her milk had dried up.

"I'm off to school," said Spike one morning,

stamping hard on the flapping plaster that was wound around his shoe to keep the sole on. His mother was in bed. Her head lay on the pillow next to a rusty saucepan that was catching rainwater as it dripped through a hole in the roof. "Have we got anything for tea?"

"Take some money from my purse," whispered his mother. But the purse was empty.

"It's OK," he said, as angry tears of helplessness welled up in her eyes. "I get paid tonight. I'll buy something to eat on the way home."

"You're a good boy," she said, "going out to work after school."

"It's only a couple of hours, and three pounds is three pounds!" smiled Spike. His mother's face was pale and worn. "I'm sorry," she coughed. "If I could wave a magic wand and make our life better, I would." But she couldn't.

When Spike climbed out of the trailer and set off for school he forgot to close the door behind him. It thumped against the aluminium panel and woke his mother from a fitful sleep. She raised a weary eye as a crouching shadow scuttled into the galley. Outside, Ruby mooed at the long brown tail as it slunk through the door and was snatched out of view by a claw.

Spike worked for a ladies' hairdresser. Every day after school he swept the cut hair off the floor and made cups of tea for the customers. On this particular day, business was slack. The only customer was an eleven-year-old girl called Esmerelda, a self-obsessed madam with a loud mouth and big hair who came in seven days a week. She had a huge blonde mane that tumbled down her back to her knees. It was thick and glossy like the coat of an Afghan hound. It was that bouncy sort of hair you see toothy girls tossing this way and that in shampoo commercials. It was teased and tousled and scrunched and puffed into a mountain of artificiality that was held together with starch and glue.

Esmerelda, you see, was entering the annual Miss Golden Locks competition down on the pier, a competition of the utmost import to all the fluffy-headed young ladies of the town. In addition to winning fifty pounds and having her picture on the front page of the *Evening Argos*, the winner also booked her place on a float in the summer parade with dogs from the RSPCA hospital, and won herself a chance to try out as a real fashion model. Esmerelda had to win at all costs. Being a model had been her lifelong ambition ever since she was eight and a half. As a result she spent twenty-five pounds a day at the hairdresser, having scientific lotions and potions poured on to her crowning glory in order to lengthen and strengthen each individual strand of hair. Failure was not an option for Esmerelda. If she didn't win Miss Golden Locks she had vowed to shave her head and go and live in a nunnery.

"Oh stop it, stop it, stop it!" she squealed as Spike swept the hair up from under her feet. "Those horrible hairs are tickling my nose. Go away, monkey boy! I'm here to be made beautiful and all you're doing is making me sneeze."

Spike looked forlorn. Although he never expected a girl as ravishingly beautiful as

Esmerelda to like him, he harboured a sneaky hope that she might.

"Sorry," he mumbled, as she turned back to the mirror and wittered to the bored girl who was cutting her hair.

"Of course, Sandra, I don't think a man is a real man unless his body is covered in waves of thick glossy hair." Sandra pulled a face.

"Not all over. Yuck!"

"And *you* a girl who works with hair!" Esmerelda's shriek was as shrill as a referee's whistle. She was eleven years old, but was trying to sound thirty. "Oh, that's so darlingly funny!" Then suddenly her laugh cut out. "What are you doing?"

Sandra was pouring a dollop of pink cream into the palm of her hand. "I'm nourishing your follicles," she said defensively.

"With Nowtincide Complex?" Esmerelda checked nervously.

"Of course."

"And added Gulli-girl-gluten with Cost-a-bob-or-twolin?" Sandra nodded.

"Because I need my chemicals, Sandra. My

hair has to be stronger and longer than anyone else's or I'll never be Miss Golden Locks!"

"Tea?" smiled Spike, offering a mug to the girl of his dreams. "One sugar, just the way you like it."

"Oh, go away, you insensitive brute!" bawled the big-haired brat in the chair, knocking the hot tea over Spike's trousers. "Can't you see I'm preening!"

Spike stood very still, waiting for the hot liquid to soak into his thigh – but before the pain arrived the door burst open and Esmerelda's parents screeched in. Their 4x4 thrummed outside on a double yellow line, while the labradors barked in the boot.

"Fury!" shouted her purple-faced father.

"And grave disappointment," added her frowning mother. "These are the emotions that are currently troubling your father and me."

"Oh, go away!" screeched their bee-hived daughter.

"But we have forbidden you to come in here every day."

"Not being a natural beauty yourself,

mother," said Esmerelda shockingly, "you wouldn't understand. Beauty has to be worked at and maintained."

"Like a boiler," said Spike supportively.

Esmerelda glowered.

"Sorry."

"But Goldilocks," simpered her mother, "Mummy's only concerned that all those chemicals will ruin your beautiful hair."

"What would happen if they turned it green?" asked her father.

"If the chemicals turned my hair green, I would dye it back again. There's nothing you can say to dissuade me. I *will* have the most beautiful hair in the world and there's an end to it!"

But there was not an end to it, because for once, her soft-as-a-brush parents would not be disobeyed. "I'm sorry Esmerelda, but prepare yourself for a cruel blow. . ."

"Agh!" Spike's sudden scream interrupted the mother's sentence like a fire alarm. The hot tea had just reached his skin and he jumped around the shop like a morris dancer in a wasp's nest.

"You're coming home with us!"

Esmerelda knew when she was beaten. "You're poos!" she sulked, jumping out of the chair. "And will my *jailers* allow me to tend to my burnt boyfriend before they drag me away?"

Boyfriend! Spike's eyeballs pinged out on red alert. Boyfriend! Were those angels he could hear? And why had his leg suddenly stopped hurting?

"Boyfriend!" he gasped.

"Shut up," hissed Esmerelda as she pushed the limply swooning Spike into a back room and whispered urgently into his ear. "Look, I'm sorry if everything I've ever said to you has made it sound like I hate you," she stated bluntly, "but the truth is that I think you're very handsome and I fancy you nearly as much as I'm crazy about peanut butter."

Spike pinched his own skinny arm to check he wasn't dreaming.

"Is this love?" he asked.

She took a moment to respond. "It might be," she schemed, offering just enough hope to keep Spike interested.

He grinned foolishly. "And might *might be* ever be *is*?"

"If you steal the chemical shampoo and bring it to my house, it might. But it must contain Nowtincide, Gulli-girl-gluten and Cost-a-bob-or-twolin, or it won't do. Comprendo? Bring me that and I *might* love you."

And then she was gone, twirling out of his life in a whirlwind of curls like a cunning blonde-widow spider.

Spike was caught on the horns of a dilemma. Stealing was wrong, but if it meant that Esmerelda might love him, surely it was worth being just a tiny bit bad? It wasn't really a dilemma. He waited till Sandra had gone out the back to freshen up for the bus-ride home before sweeping half a dozen shampoos into a carrier bag and covering them with hair cuttings to avoid discovery.

When he got home he was all a-tingle with passionate anticipation. He took a shower underneath the overspill pipe that drained water off the flyover and dried himself on a sheet of newspaper. When he was dressed again he took out the stolen shampoo and admired it, just as other suitors might admire a diamond ring or a Fabergé necklace.

As he laid the bottle back down on the hair cuttings, however, he suddenly remembered what his beloved Esmerelda had said to Sandra about *real men* and *body hair*. So he rushed down the road to a builder's skip, retrieved a pot of lumpy wallpaper paste, painted himself all over and stuck on the loose hair from the plastic bag. In less than half an hour, Spike was a hairy man – just what Esmerelda liked!

"Spike!"

Spike clamped his shirt across his chest so that his mother wouldn't see the hair.

"Mum," he said. "What are you doing out of bed?"

She was standing in the doorway to the caravan.

"After you left this morning," she said, "I had a visitor." Her voice was bubbling. There was a twinkle in her eye. "He was a hobgoblin, or so he said. A little monkey-man all covered in hair with a big bony head. Apparently he heard me wish for a wish this morning and came in to grant it."

Spike was having difficulty keeping up.

"How do you know he was a hobgoblin?"

"He showed me his card, like the gasman used to. It said: *Geraldo the Lawngrower, Hobgoblin and Hex-Horticulturist*. He gave us this." She held out a hessian sack with the top folded back. Inside there was grass seed. "It's magic," she giggled. "He told me to plant one seed in the window-box every night, water it and wait till the morning when it will have grown into a huge blade of grass."

"Is that good?" asked Spike.

"Good!" laughed his mother. "Ruby can eat the grass and produce milk. And milk we can *sell*! It's a miracle!"

Spike was pleased that his mother was pleased. He gave her a hug.

"I'll be back before it's dark," he said, as she untangled her arms and bent down to plant the first seed.

"There is one thing you should know," she

added, matter-of-factly. "We must only ever plant one seed at a time. Planting more is highly dangerous and should be avoided." Spike nodded absent-mindedly and turned to go, but his mother's voice stopped him. "Spike!" She was standing now with a puzzled look on her face. "Haven't you grown up quickly?" she said. "Time was when you didn't have one hair on your body, but now . . . gosh, it's a forest!"

Spike blushed, picked up the stolen shampoo and ran off down the road, his hairy chest rustling under his shirt like a family of ferrets scampering through bracken.

But when Esmerelda saw Spike in all his hairiness she screamed and screamed and screamed and screamed. Her face turned bright purple and she started to pant. She thought he was a monkey in boys' clothes and monkeys were bad news for people with big hair, because monkeys liked to rummage through hair looking for lice! Spike had to pull all the hair off in front of her to prove it wasn't real.

"It's me, Spike!" he cried. "I was only trying to be sexy."

But Spike trying to be sexy had reduced Esmerelda to a neurotic jelly. Her parents found her quivering on the floor when they burst into the room.

"Screaming!" shouted her father. "That's what I heard." Spike had crawled under the bed and was holding his breath.

"And hair!" screeched her mother. "On the floor. That's what I'm seeing!"

"There were long-haired rats in here," lied Esmerelda. "That's why I screamed. And when they heard you coming in, they were so scared that they jumped out of their skins. That's the hair."

"You're weird," stated her father, clinically. "Those shampoo chemicals are scrambling your brain, Esmerelda. There it is, I've said it." And with that he was gone.

"I do wish you'd listen to your father," whispered Esmerelda's mother. "He's a wise man, he reads a book every year, and if he says the chemicals are bad for you they must be."

And with that *she* was gone, allowing Spike to crawl out from under the bed and grin sheepishly.

"Sorry," he winced. "I thought the hairy chest would be acceptable."

"You clumsy oaf!" she blubbed. "My gorgeous hair was *that* close to losing volume. If I had lapsed into hysteria, I might have pulled it out by the handful!"

Spike really was sorry and handed over the bag of stolen shampoo by way of a peace offering, but all that did was rekindle her fury. Fresh tears bubbled up from her boots.

"They're not all here!" she wailed. "You've forgotten the shampoo with Nowtincide!"

Poor Spike. His first date was going down the toilet.

"I did my best," he said softly. "I stole what I could."

"And it wasn't good enough!" seethed the brat with the bouffant. "If I don't win Miss Golden Locks, *you* will be to blame!"

"Do you not love me then?" he asked.

She fixed him with a cold and cruel stare.

"Well, you obviously don't love *me* or you'd have got me what I asked for. Steal me the shampoo with Nowtincide and I'll let you know."

And that was as much encouragement as Spike was going to get.

He woke up the following morning feeling awful. Not only was he a thief, but he had let down Esmerelda as well. He wanted to go back to sleep, but his mother wouldn't let him.

"Come and see," she trilled. "The magic grass seed has grown. Ruby's eating!"

And true enough, when Spike went outside and squinted into the sunshine, there was the cow chewing a huge blade of lush, green grass from the window-box.

Spike was crushed in his mother's arms. "Oh Spike, I'm so happy," she beamed. "Our troubles are over!"

It is a sad fact that when one says positively, "Our troubles are over!" they never actually are. When Spike turned up for work after school, Sandra met him in the doorway.

"Don't bother coming in here," she said coldly. "I thought I could trust you, Spike. I thought you needed the work to look after your poor mother, but obviously I was wrong. Thieves are not welcome in my shop. You're fired!" Then the door was slammed in his face.

Spike wondered what he should do. He decided to be honest.

With a heavy heart he trudged round to Esmerelda's house.

"I'm sorry," he said. "I tried, but I couldn't get that shampoo with Nowtincide."

"Then how am I going to win Miss Golden Locks!" she screamed, kicking Spike hard in the knee. "I need my chemicals. I must have big hair! I must have the longest, thickest hair in the whole wide world!"

"Wait here," said Spike as a cunning grin spread across his face. He'd just had the sort of idea that Einstein must have had when people called him a genius.

Spike rushed home to find his mother sitting on two up-ended bricks in the sunshine. She was milking Ruby and singing while she pulled on the udders.

"Look Spike," she cried. "Our first milk in a month! Isn't it a beautiful day?"

But Spike was in too much of a hurry to reply. He dashed inside the caravan, snatched up the sack of magic grass seed and was gone.

"You must eat it," he explained to a sceptical Esmerelda, who was sniffing the seed sack suspiciously. "Then drink a couple of pints of water and wait for the seeds to grow."

"This is a joke, isn't it?"

"It's magic!" said Spike. "It worked for a cow, why shouldn't it work for you?" He could have put that better. "It's magic, Esmerelda. Trust me. If you want the longest, thickest hair in the world, eat one."

"But my hair will be green."

"So dye it!" said Spike. "That's what you told your parents you'd do."

"Oh, all right!" she squealed gleefully, scooping a handful of seeds out of the sack.

"Careful," warned Spike. "You must only

take one. Eating more is highly dangerous and should be avoided."

"Nonsense," said Esmerelda. "The more seeds I eat, the more luscious my locks will be."

"But the hobgoblin said. . ."

"You don't believe in hobgoblins, do you?" she scoffed. "Grow up, Spike!" And with that she picked up the whole sack and poured every last grass seed down her throat.

"Do you love me now?" asked Spike.

"Ask me again in the morning," she replied cagily, "when we see if it's worked."

When Spike got home, Ruby looked miserable and his mother had gone back to bed.

"Oh Spike!" she cried as he came through the door. "A most terrible thing has happened." Spike tried not show that he knew. "The magic grass seed has been stolen! What are we going to do?"

"We'll look for it in the morning," he said, avoiding eye-contact with his mother. "I wonder who could have done it?" But she did not reply. She was sobbing.

Spike climbed into bed with a fist of guilt lodged firmly in the pit of his stomach.

The next morning, Spike was woken by a furious knocking on the door. He opened it to find Esmerelda standing outside, jabbering with excitement. On top of her head was a shock of startling green grass that circled her ears like a huge halo, plunged to the ground and fluttered behind her like a wedding veil.

"Who is it?" croaked Spike's mother, half-waking in her bed.

"No one," said Spike, scared lest his mother should guess where the grass seed had gone. He pushed Esmerelda away from the door and jumped outside to join her.

"I'm going to win Miss Golden Locks!" she crowed ecstatically. "When I've finished with the peroxide I shall have the most beautiful blonde hair in the world. The other girls will be so jealous. They'll be crying all over the place, but that won't bother me, because I'll have won and they'll just be pathetic nothings with floor mops for hair!"

Spike was going to ask Esmerelda if she loved him *now*, but the words were snatched off his tongue by the freaky sight of her arms and legs.

"Oh hairy hobgoblins!" he gasped. "Look what's happening!"

She looked down and squeaked. The grass was still growing. Tiny green shoots were wriggling out of her skin like peppermint worms. They were sprouting all over her body.

"Help!" she whimpered, but Spike had no cure for magic. The grass grew on, covering her face like a lost golf ball in the rough, swamping her body, flowing out across the yard like a deep, green river. And when it reached Ruby she did what any hungry cow would do. She ate it. She gobbled up the grass *and* the ghastly girl inside it, faster than it takes a startled boy to cry out, "Whoops!"

Spike didn't move for several seconds. When he did, he laughed with relief. Now that the grass seed was where it was meant to be all along – inside the cow – he didn't feel quite so bad about stealing it. Besides, Esmerelda was not really his type of girl. She was a bit grassy for him!

Ruby mooed, causing Spike to look round for the second shock in as many minutes. Because the magic seeds were inside Esmerelda and Esmerelda was now inside the cow, the cow had also grown a lawn. Ruby's two stomachs rumbled appreciatively. She was in seventh heaven. Her skin was covered in thick, green grass and although she never produced another drop of milk, she *did* become the most famous freak cow in the world.

"Roll up, roll up! Forget your boring Moo Cows, see the one and only Mow Cow. The only known herbivore who can eat herself!"

Spike and his mother travelled with Ruby from country to country attracting crowds wherever they went. Small children played football on Ruby's back and several Hollywood directors used her to advertise butter. Which meant, of course, that Spike and his mother never had to worry about money again.